Gauri Deshpande is a well-known writer and translator. Known for her bold themes and innovative writing in Marathi, she has published poems, essays and short stories in English as well. Her translation of the sixteen volumes of Sir Richard Burton's *The Arabian Nights* is considered a landmark event in Marathi publishing history. She also teaches postgraduate courses in English Literature at the University of Poona. This is her first collection of short stories in English.

The Lackadaisical Sweeper

Short Stories by
GAURI DESHPANDE

MĀNAS

MANAS, an imprint of
EastWest Books (Madras) Pvt. Ltd.

62-A, Ormes Road, Kilpauk, Chennai 600 010
3-5-1108, Narayanaguda, Hyderabad 500 029
239,DMM Building, Chamarajpet, Bangalore 560 018

Distributors:
Rupa & Co
15, Bankim Chatterjee Street, Calcutta 700 073
135, South Malaka, Allahabad 211 011
P G Solanki Path, Lamington Road, Mumbai 400 007
7/16, Ansari Road, Daryaganj, New Delhi 110 002

© 1997 Gauri Deshpande

ISBN: 81-86852-04-2

Price: Rs.135/-

Cover painting by Dakshinamoorthy C
Cover design by Sanka Graphics

Typeset by Kalyani Rajaraman, Alwarpet, Chennai 600 018
Printed by Sri Venkatesa Printing House, Chennai 600 026

Published by EastWest Books (Madras) Pvt. Ltd.,
62-A, Ormes Road, Kilpauk, Chennai 600 010

Many of the stories in this collection first appeared in *Satyakatha, Mouj, Saptahik Sakal, Stree, Deepavali, The Illustrated Weekly of India, PEN, Debonair, Times Weekly* and other journals in India and abroad.

Contents

Hookworm, Lamprey, Tick, Fluke and Flea	1
The Lackadaisical Sweeper	13
Hello, Stranger!	29
A Harmless Girl	43
Map	54
Whatever Happened to...	63
Smile and Smile and...	74
The Debt	86
Insy Winsy Spider	118
Vervain	126
Rose Jam	141
Morgan in Disguise	163
Dmitri in the Afternoon	175
Habits	187
Brand New Pink Nikes	195
Afterword	207

Hookworm, Lamprey, Tick, Fluke and Flea

THE whole lot of us heaved a collective sigh of relief when the Corvelhos finally emigrated to Canada. The endless farewell parties at which Tony got predictably drunk and lecherous, and Jenny got just as predictably whiney and lachrymose were beginning to bring us dangerously close to the brink. None of us, however, had the heart or the guts to stay away. We all gathered at one another's houses and ate the same food, drank the same cocktails, said the same things and displayed the same feelings. I even went so far as to wear the same clothes, but then they were all used to me by now.

I had been the first one to give up on Jenny, the first one to close my door to Tony and the first one to refuse to baby-sit Brian, Nathan and Emilion. I was, also quite predictably, the only one to refrain from shedding tears at their departure.

It seemed to me that we could now close this painful chapter in our lives. In fact, I thought, we could now disband and begin to live our separate lives at last. For quite a number of years we seemed to have been bound together willy-nilly by Jenny and Tony and Brian and Nathan and Emilion. Why else would a bunch of women with nothing in common but a dimly remembered classroom, stick together into ripe maturity? Over the years, we had got into the habit of holding interminable and inconclusive consultations about Jenny. Never a day went by but we were on the phone to 'discuss' Jenny. And of course, any one discussion or conversation had to be relayed to all others by the participants. You can imagine the endless permutations and combinations of that round robin. But in the beginning of course, were Jenny and Tony.

Of us, she was the first to get married. Right out of high school; at a crucial time when we were about to scatter—some to college, some to art schools, some into jobs, some just waiting around for their turn at matrimony. As Mala said, 'We would all have flown away, had not Jenny and Tony cast their net of enchantment over us!' She tended to say things like that and so it was no surprise to any of us that she found a niche in copywriting to come up with unforgettable gems in the service of teas and talcs. We were all a bit uneasy about Tony from the start. Ratna and I had not, prior to Tony, been exposed to 'their' sort of people, meaning Indian Catholics from Goa (Jenny, after all, was born and brought up in the same suburb of Bombay as the rest of us); so we thought an alarming tendency on his part towards consumption of alcohol—which we had never even seen before—and his habit of trying to put his arms around us, were part of his different cultural background.

However, Mala, Shama, Aysha and Amrita had known 'such people' before and they assured us that Tony was an exception. They rightly pointed out how none of Jenny's brothers or brothers-in-law did those things.

Also, Aysha said, 'Ethnic minorities restrict peculiarly ethnic behaviour to the in-group, presenting a generally acceptable and conformist politeness to the world at large.' It was no surprise either that she ended up a professor of sociology and that Tony ended up a major lush and Lothario. The entirety of his unpleasant characteristics took some time to surface because he hid them under what he thought was charm. Each of us according to our various leanings took steps to protect ourselves from him. Aysha and Shama acquired husbands who defended them from other males as husbands are supposed to do. Salim even punched out Tony once and Aysha, a pleased spectator of her husband's prowess, explained the dumbstruck reaction of the rest of us by saying, 'The majority's interest generally restricts itself to the role of bystander when different minorities fight it out among themselves.' I wondered if she would have called it an unreasonable show of force by the majority if *I* had hauled off and hit Tony as I was so often tempted to do. In fact, I never actually hit him, because every time the occasion arose, I was in two minds about whom to hit first, him or Jenny.

It is seldom, if ever, that pity is not accompanied by condescension towards the object of it. Mistrusting my pity for Jenny therefore, I took refuge in furious rejection and made scathing remarks about lying in beds which one had made oneself. The other five had more charity or more leisure or more altruism or more optimism or more something; as a result of which they were continuously plagued by Jenny's not infrequent and often hysterical forays into their lives.

I heard about the time she parked in Mala's house for a month, the time she embarrassed Aysha in the staff-room by bursting into tears, the time she threw herself into Shama's arms, rendering her unfit for morning puja, and the time the large-hearted but one-roomed Ratna was woken up by her at midnight, one horrible brat in each arm.

I began to discern hints about my special qualifications for standing godmother to Jenny and her atrocious sons. I was the only one who had not married and produced consumers to deplete further the store of earth's limited resources. As the years had lengthened and all of them had acquired these appendages, their distress at Jenny's periodic demands on their time, money, space and sympathy had become more acute and so had the pressure on me to take her over. At last, around the time she was expecting the last horror to be born, and I was approached once again, I decided to Take A Stand. Tony had again lost his job, was drinking heavily, and was beating up on her and the boys. Aysha's daughter had measles, Ratna's parents-in-law had come to stay, Mala's husband was gearing up for C.A. finals, Shama was herself in the all-the-time-sick stage of pregnancy and Amrita's husband had been overcome by sudden deafness when Jenny was mentioned.

I called a council of war. I served coffee to the non-pregnant ones, alka seltzer to the slightly pregnant one, a tot of rum to myself. (I had progressed far since the days when I had never even seen any.) Then I said that old Jenny and her problems were really bugging us and a—I could not help but call it that—final solution had to be reached. They concurred. I said, 'Let us first delineate our goals and then explore avenues that might lead to them.' (It had come as no surprise to anyone that I became a systems analyst.) They concurred again. 'The first of Jenny's problems is Tony.' Agreement. 'So we must get rid of him.' Alarm. 'She must divorce him.' Panic. Religious objections. Indignation on my side. 'Ok, then leave the divorce. Just let her get out.' Qualified acquiescence. 'She must have a tubectomy because she must not produce any more horrible children if she has to get a job of sorts to support herself and these useless men she has already accumulated.'

Great perturbation and more religious objections. Furious outburst from me, accompanied by use of unsuitable language. Soothing noises from the non-pregnant ones, as my attitude was considered deleterious to the wellbeing of the slightly pregnant one. Icy calm on my part. 'All right. Here is the bottom line. Unless Jenny gets rid of Tony for good, shows me a certificate of tubectomy and sends the two older horrors far away to some sort of an educational institution (preferably correctional), I will have nothing to do with her. If you guys try to take advantage of the fact that I am the only one among you with the strength of character to keep variations of the Tonys, Brians and Nathans out of my life, I will have no more to do with you either. Bring me Jenny with her about-to-be born baby and I undertake to find her houseroom and gainful employment but bring me all five as a package, and you can keep them.'

There was an uneasy silence after this announcement and a couple of the non-pregnant ones gingerly helped themselves to some alcohol as well. Finally Aysha said, 'The helplessness of half-educated, middle class, urban, Indian females, in the face of marital problems could be the subject of an important study.' Mala chipped in with, 'One is Aghast at How the Flower of Indian Womanhood is Withering on the Vine.' I thought to warn them before they left gloomily that if they persisted in their misguided notions of beneficence, they were likely to put a strain on the vines, trees, branches and flowers of their own marriages and families which were showing definite signs of withering; but merely contented myself with telling Aysha to let me have a copy of her study when it was completed, and Mala to think up more slogans for instant coffee that would steady the nerves of the Flower of Indian Womanhood.

Jenny herself never approached me after the time, early on, when I refused to tolerate either her drunken husband or her imaginatively destructive children in my home. Whenever I met her in the houses of other friends, she always said a few hopeful things about Tony's new job and her sons' new school (both changed with great frequency as most people's tolerance level for the Corvelhos was low) and busied herself vainly in preventing the one from making drunken passes at the female guests and the others from wrecking the hostess' audio or video systems. I saw the sons growing into great big layabouts like their father and Jenny growing brittle and small and shrivelled.

I continued to get regular 'progress' reports from the Kind-hearted Quintet about her continuing misfortunes and always renewed my offer of hospitality provided she got rid of the Corvelho Chamber Orchestra and came to me solo.

Then I had to leave town for a few months, and in my absence, a Canadian cousin was discovered for the Corvelhos by Aysha who had met him during one of her international seminars. This poor man had been away so long that he was either unaware of or had forgotten the extent of the disaster area his cousins represented. He agreed to sponsor their immigration when first Aysha and then, bullied by her, the rest of us assured him that their departure and resettlement would be financed and that four strong, hulking men would quickly find work in labour-short Canada.

Because of the ways in which the Canadian government moves mysteriously its wonders to perform, such totally unsuitable recipients of immigrant status did receive it and everyone pitched in and gave them warm clothes and farewell parties and bought their dilapidated furniture and pretended to be heartbroken and uttered promises of visits and parted with cash and arranged their freight and passages cheaply through friends, colleagues and acquaintances, and, as I said at the beginning, heaved a collective sigh of relief when they finally left.

After a few weeks I received a proper note of thanks from Jenny, enclosing a photograph of her four large men practically obscuring a small, two-storey wooden house with a maple in the front yard. The others got longer letters, giving glowing details of life in Canada: reunions with philanthropic cousins, godsends of generous friends, introductions to hospitable neighbours, acquisitions of lucrative jobs and enrolments at accommodating schools. She herself seemed to be a lady of leisure, what with all the latest gadgets and appliances bought on credit, the ready-to-eat frozen dinners and the enticing, twenty-four hour TV. In all the letters, there were profuse thanks for our help; but when I pointed out that there were no offers of repayment, I was shouted down as a veritable Scrooge.

In the next few months I got nary a call from the Eleemosynary Ensemble because one cannot really dilate as satisfactorily upon happiness and success as upon misery. As the bleak Canadian winter approached, there was silence for a long time, and then the portentous announcement: Jenny was coming home.

The phones buzzed busily and plans were made and sad-but-brave-and-hopeful voices announced the Beginning of a New Era. I was prevailed upon to offer her a home since the boys were not accompanying her and she had obviously left Tony and presumably was not in need of a tubectomy. So I waived that clause and gave in and found her on my doorstep around one a.m. one morning in early December. I welcomed her in and showed her the guest room and assured her that the others would be rushing in at daybreak, as soon as she was a little rested and over her jet-lag. Actually, they all gathered round for lunch.

Coming out of the kitchen to say 'grub's up!' I checked on the threshold, suddenly seeing the whole bunch together, sort of larger-than-life and in sharper focus. I was amazed to see how we were all so changed and yet so much the same.

Aysha, the plumpest by far, and also the most successful if rank and renown were to be the yardstick, the youngest head of department in the university. Mala, who had never managed to lose all the gains of three quick pregnancies, was not fat but a big, buxom, fashionably dressed matron, financially the best off, a partner now in her ad agency. Ratna and Amrita, with the regulation 'hum do humare do' families, losing the battle of the bulge, with time on their hands, paying lip-service to Lib and talking of rejoining the workforce. Shama, now divorced and single-parenting a teenager, juggling job, parenthood, selfhood, friendships; gaunt of face and flabby of muscle. I, thin through endless counting of calories, yet hiding in big, baggy clothes and needing to bolster my ego by using the occult jargon of my trade to interest, awe and mystify.

And then there was Jenny : small, straight, slim, short-haired, smart, full of laughter and pleased to be the centre of attention. Every sentence contained some reference to her 'boys', such as: 'I insisted my boys repaint the house when they were between jobs,' or 'I make my boys sweep up and burn the leaf-litter, so they are always threatening to cut down the maple, but you can bet on its being there next autumn,' or 'my boys knocked down the wall between the box room and the hall-closet last summer and we now have a neat little guest room,' or 'when the boys are home on weekends, our house is like a fairground, they are so popular,' or 'they run me off my feet, my boys do,' or 'my boys are all working now so they thought they'd buy me a present—a ticket home. I sure needed a holiday and so I said, Why don't I come and visit with you all?'

This last brought us up short and cut off various commiserating or encouraging sentences in mid-syllable. We stared at her. Jenny was here simply on a holiday, thank you. She was in no trouble, had not given up 'her boys', did not want a job, nor Liberation. She was thrilled to bits to be who, what and where she was: an unpaid slave to those four useless, worthless, penniless drunkards and wastrels. She adored them and lay herself down to be trampled on; she wore herself out to supply their every need, she worked herself to the bone to support them, she was happy to be digging herself into an early grave...

We continued to stare at her. Small, straight, bright, slim, crop-haired, smart, full of laughter...

She was nowhere near an early grave; if at all, far further than any of us. We were worn to the bone being her unpaid slaves, supplying her every need, laying ourselves down to be trampled on and paying our huge telephone bills.

Without realizing it, the Stupid Samaritans had stood up and gravitated towards me. There we were all, the short and the tall and the thin and the fat and the rich and the poor and the smart and the shabby. She said, 'I can't tell you how much I owe you all! Where would my boys and I be without you? Nowhere!'

Indeed we believed her.

The Lackadaisical Sweeper

THE pavement pounders crawl out of beds and hit the streets in Hong Kong the same as in any other city. They come in all shapes, sizes, colours and speeds. But even the smallest, slowest and least enthusiastic of them—specifications that easily fit Seeta—could not have failed to fall over the street sweeper. He was low on the ground, about the height of a good-sized Great Dane, and hunchbacked to boot. He was so slow he practically stood still and his enthusiasm was so markedly absent that the street looked the same when he left as when he arrived. He was also surly and ignored the cheery 'good morning' tossed at him by the strollers, dog-walkers, race-walkers, joggers and runners.

It would not have occurred to Seeta to say 'good morning' to a street cleaner in her native

Bangalore (where they were an invisible breed anyhow), because everyone, he included, would have thought it irrelevant. She certainly had no hang-ups about sweepers belonging to, well, the sweeper caste, because she had been brought up right by liberal, post-Independence parents. Her father and grandfather were members of the 'Caste Eradication Society', and her mother had taught her never to raise her voice to a servant. Their espousal of the eradication of caste had not led them to find spouses—either for themselves or their children—outside of their own caste, but then one had to be realistic. Some things were simply not done.

Her marriage, arranged by both sets of parents, was exactly what pleased everyone. Her husband was educated, good-looking, and on a longish foreign posting. And most important, his people were reasonable in their demands, asking for no more than, as her father put it, the traffic could bear. The only slight disappointment she knew was when Narain wrote 'Seeta' in the heap of grain with the diamond ring her father had given him as a present. She had wanted a fashionable new name, but Narain said, 'Seeta' was the epitome of wifely virtue, so why should he change it? She thought this a frivolous argument, because, whatever her name, she was bound to try and excel at wifely virtues.

It was in pursuance of that goal that she mingled in the mornings with the pavement smoothers of Hong Kong and encountered the lackadaisical sweeper. The fact was, she had always been plump; a plump little dimpled baby and a plump girl and was now a plump young woman. This was as it should be, because no husband wants a skinny scarecrow for his wife. But soon after marriage, she got plumper and people began to ask if she were pregnant. As she was not, and as Narain wouldn't hear of a baby 'for at least three years', she wondered if he would not like her to lose some weight. Skinny women seemed to be admired in these parts. When consulted on this, as on all topics, Narain said carelessly, she should go for a walk after he left for work.

So she did go out the next morning, and was amazed to see the quiet residential street leading to the beach from their apartment thronged with enthusiastic rubber-scorchers. She was inundated with good mornings, a lovely day for a walk, phew, it's hot, and that is one great outfit, and did not quite know what was expected in return, because, though her English was perfectly adequate, it did not run to meaningless small talk. A smile seemed to be enough at the beginning, until very soon she too was tossing out good mornings with the best of them, even, to her own surprise, at the street cleaner, who never looked up.

She was happy to think she was burning off some unwanted fat, and relieved to have something to do other than redundant housework in the mornings. After all, how many times can one clean a spotless small flat or wash and iron spanking clean sheets and shirts? But now, thanks to Narain's directive, her empty mornings were filled with activity.

The second week into her leisurely morning walks, she met a kindred soul—as laggardly, unenthusiastic and willing to while away the morning as herself—Sheila. Visibly pregnant and visibly and audibly American; large, tall, vigorous, voluble, bonhomous, blond and with a mouth full of the most enormous, perfectly regular and white teeth Seeta had ever seen. As the slowest slugs of the low-impact aerobic squad, they naturally fell in step and discovered that they lived in the same apartment building. Within the next two hours Seeta would have come to know all she ever wanted about Sheila's life and times, thoughts and emotions, disappointments and orgasms if only she had been able to follow more than fifty per cent of what was being said. First of all, she had difficulty in hearing the continuous rumbling going on a foot above her ear. Second, the accent was unlike anything she had encountered before. And third, she was not always sure of the meanings of words and phrases used. For instance, she deciphered 'the thumbie in the wombie was all a mistake', but hadn't a clue how 'Jake likes his cushion, back and front, but he won't be able to get it up for the Fat Man' could be an explanation of why Sheila was out early, walking reluctantly in the sixth month of her unwanted pregnancy.

Naturally shy, she was a bit alarmed by this reckless generosity of spirit, wondering if reciprocity were expected. But it was soon apparent that Sheila, simply a generous soul, wanted only to give. Nothing in her eyes was too trivial or insignificant to share with a new-found friend. And Seeta began to see, albeit vaguely, that Sheila's talk mostly consisted of intimate and historical details of her life, mainly with her husband Jake.

When some of these conversations were relayed to Narain, he laughed and said, 'Seems like a card, this 'friend' of yours. Why not find out what her husband does? Might be useful.'

She did not know what he meant by 'useful', because she did not fathom exactly what he did. Was it banking, shares and bonds, or real estate? Something to do with Money, and she hadn't the remotest about money with a capital M. Of course she was smart and educated; but her B.A. was in home science. Experience had shown it was very useful in getting a husband. So she could also see that degrees and such could be termed 'useful'. But could friends be 'useful'?

She suppressed this thought as she suspected it of not being in keeping with wifely virtues, and the very next morning, taking advantage of Sheila's being a bit breathless on an upgrade, asked her what Jake did. Sheila laughed on the downslope and said, 'Hey, I didn't tell you? He's an airline steward, the bum.' This was a new word, Seeta noted, in reference to Jake, whom his wife variously called, with affection and pride: hunk, hose, maniac, dummy, flake, loverboy. Names like Blackford and Sleeping Bull, the significance of which escaped her, had also appeared.

Narain's reaction to this harmless occupation of Jake's was surprising. 'An airline steward! You're not serious. Will you tell me how they can afford to stay in this building? Even in this area? Airline steward! Trust you to pick the one woman in that crowd who is perfectly useless!' Stung by his contempt, the earlier rebel-thought came back : friends went to the same school, lived on the same street, came one's way through family. Whether any of them, made more through destiny than choice, were 'useful' or not was not a qualifying condition. They were friends; that was enough.

This was the first time she had found a friend all on her own, though the only thing she had in common with her was her gait. In spite of Narain's demand to know how Jake could afford to stay in so posh an area on so lowly a salary, she did not like to ask, for she was brought up to assume money was made by men in the pursuit of some profession or the other, and one never asked how or how much. But it wasn't necessary to ask Sheila any questions. Information came forth from her in large instalments. Seeta soon heard that Jake and Sheila occupied Sheila's 'Dad's pad'. 'Dad' had had the foresight just after the war, when he found himself in the Far East with a bit of bread, to invest in real estate, which was now outtasight, right?

In the midst of this slightly arcane explanation, Sheila suddenly stopped and said, 'Honey, you know, I am just totally determined to see the Humpback of Notre Dame smile before I quit the shoe dragging.' Thinking this new name yet another tribute to some unfathomable talent of the much-admired-and-much-maligned Jake, Seeta asked, surprised, 'You mean Jake does not smile at you?' Baffled, Sheila said, 'What!' And then catching the misunderstanding, let out a guffaw and added, 'Oh, no! That shark is always smiling with all his teeth. I mean this midget. This surly pygmy...Good mornin', little Chang.' She bared her own array of large, white teeth at the sweeper hunched over his broom amid fallen petals of bauhinias, empty soy-milk cartons, crushed Marlboro packs, soiled tissue papers and dog turds. He didn't notice them.

That evening Narain discussed the matter of Sheila's Dad's pad and her lifestyle with a couple of colleagues who had come for dinner: 'Dad's bread' might set up the young couple in a flat hereabouts but Jake needed a steady supply of a lot more to continue here. 'Wonder what scam he's pulling?' Narain winked and laughed, and the rest shared the joke. But Seeta was puzzled and asked one of the women who said a little condescendingly, 'You know! All these stewards and stewardesses are always into smuggling.'

This answer did not satisfy Seeta. She knew they smuggled a bit of this and that. At home, foreign make-up, perfume, the bottle of Scotch her father produced on special occasions had no doubt come from a 'friend of a friend of a friend' who was a steward. But how much money could be made out of such things in a place like Hong Kong where everything and its imitation was sold openly? When she said this, the woman laughed and said, 'Oh, don't be so naive,' but did not elaborate, and later on, remarked to her husband on their way home that Seeta was a typical small-town girl. 'Bourgeoise' was the word she used, because her B.A. was from one of the most fashionable colleges in Delhi, and in fashionable Eng.Lit.

The very next day Sheila was sporting what looked like a small diamond in a pendant. When Seeta admired it, she said, 'Thanks, honey. And you can bet it is real! The Incredible Shrinking Man gave it to me as a consolation prize. Musta made a killing on his milk run to Bangkok. And is *that* city aptly named! But it's quite small, really, not half as big as the one you've got on your nose. Say, sweetie, whaddya do when you catch a cold?' Sheila was so pleased with her own witticism that she fortunately did not want an answer; and in any case, at just that moment, they stumbled upon Chang the street sweeper and Sheila exclaimed, 'Hey, wait a minute; I've learnt to say 'good morning' in Cantonese, can you beat it? Just for this fart!' And she called it out, but Chang, if that was indeed his name, ignored it. 'Maybe he speaks only Fuckinese,' Sheila muttered.

In the evening when Seeta asked Narain what a milk run was, he said, 'I don't know, maybe an early morning run. Why?' When Seeta told him, his eyes opened wide, and he said, 'Aren't you my clever little pussycat though? Come here!' And Seeta, had she been the sort of person who offered such confidences, would have been able to offer Sheila her newly acquired knowledge of what can be the aftermath of one's husband calling one his clever little pussycat.

A couple of days later Narain called her in the afternoon to announce that he was bringing an English colleague home for dinner. Seeta was petrified. She had never entertained an Englishman. In fact, she had never even talked to one. She was afraid she would not understand a word he said and he would look down upon her. But Graham turned out to be perfectly comprehensible. She admitted towards the end of the dinner that she had been apprehensive.

'Judging from the difficulty I have understanding Sheila...' Seeta stopped mid-sentence, but Narain picked it up and explained Sheila. She was perplexed when he encouraged her to talk about what had hitherto seemed to bore him: her friend, and at second hand, her friend's husband. She did not understand his remark about a killing in property she heard him make to Graham as she was clearing up, nor the reason for Graham's quick frown and shake of head with a glance at herself.

The next morning she recounted her adventures to Sheila, who said, 'Oh, Englishmen are kinda cute, you know. I could go for one of those in a big way.' That day she said she had learnt to say 'good morning' in Mandarin, and tried it out on the indolent and unheedful Chang with the usual result. However, she was not in the least discouraged. On the contrary, she said, she was going to keep on trying 'in all the languages of the world' until he either relented or just plain gave up and smiled. 'But why, Sheila? He doesn't care, you know.'

'Well, it's like this, honey. I like a cheerful, polite bunch of guys around me. Everybody out here has been just wonderful except this louse. I like friendly folk, like to make friends every place

I go. Imagine, I gotta Christmas card list as long as an encyclopaedia!'

Seeta could easily imagine it, because all their conversations were interrupted a hundred times by enthusiastic greetings and remarks tossed between Sheila and dozens of people who always parted with assurances of meeting soon at somebody-or-the-other's party. Seeta formed an admiring audience at these manifestations of camaraderie, but after Narain firmly and mendaciously turned down a couple of invitations from Sheila, pleading previous engagements, did not try to join in.

Once she asked Sheila what she was going to call the baby. Sheila said, 'Oh, if it's a boy, Joseph Emanuel after my dad and Jake's; and if it's a girl, Sara Ruth after our moms. I don't like those names, but what the heck, it'll please the old guys and I'll call the next one what I want.' Seeta told Narain, and he took off on an entirely different tack, saying, 'So! They are Jews, are they? Old Graham will be interested.'

This remark came as a shock to Seeta who had never before wondered if anyone was a Jew or not. But then she realized that she had never had to wonder before who anyone was. At home she always knew who everyone was, and behaved accordingly. But what did one do here? Finally she decided, this would do to start with: one should be friendly to people who were friendly in return, without worrying over their being Jews or not.

She then surprised herself by voicing this thought to Narain who was certainly surprised to find that his little pussycat of a wife not only held an opinion of her own, but actually went so far as to express it. 'That's all very well if I were about to make friends with your Sheila and Jake,' he said, 'but I'm not. I am only concerned with striking a property deal with them; and in that, my little doll, their being or not being Jews is very much to the point.' Seeta didn't always understand exactly what Narain was saying either, but his tone and the little endearment told her that he was not angry with her, regardless of her little spurt of independence, and she was relieved.

A few days later Sheila said, 'Hey, do you know, some local guy called up last night and wanted to discuss the bits of property Dad's got scattered all over old Hong Kong, but if that chink thought he could put one over old Emanuel Epstein's little girl, he had another think comin'. I mean, am I dumb to sell at these prices when everyone knows the property market's gonna go through the roof? Right? Right.'

And though uneasy at these continued references to property in connection with Sheila, Seeta did not ask her friend for an explanation. As a result of this reticence, as well as Sheila's pervasive friendliness and Seeta's real but undemanding need of a friend, their friendship prospered along with the baby in Sheila's belly. Soon, Sheila was enormous and had difficulty keeping to even so laggardly a pace as Seeta set. Laughingly she claimed to be fit to keep up only with the hunchback grouch. 'Hey Oscar, buddy, how are you?' she would call out, and reel off greetings in about ten different languages. That was the name she had bestowed on him to Seeta's mystification: Oscar Chang. He never glanced at them as they waddled past.

When it was time to begin to look forward to the arrival of Sheila's baby, Narain came home one evening in a mellow mood and told her after an unusual third whisky that he was celebrating his and Graham's having figured out how to work the whole deal. He was very pleased with her because her help had been invaluable. She was a great deal puzzled as to how she had been of any help but as usual, did not ask, content to bask in her husband's rare expression of appreciation. Later, she did feel like purring when Narain called her his little pussycat, and again, wished she could share this with Sheila, who had unstintingly, though almost always incomprehensibly, poured out so many intimate details of her own conjugal bed.

As she was putting on her shoes to go out in the morning, the doorbell rang. Peeping through the spyhole, she saw Sheila. She opened the door and before she could say more than 'Why Sheila! Is anything...?' Sheila hurriedly launched into a garbled explanation from which Seeta could only gather that she was leaving. Going home. Today. Jake was already home and in bad trouble. He needed her. 'But you can't fly now, Sheila, you are too close...' 'Oh, you don't understand, honey! I gotta get out. ASAP. But I couldn't leave without saying bye to you. I'll be all right, don't worry. Still two whole weeks before Thumbie is due out of Mummie. And besides,'—with a spurt of her usual irrepressible spirit—'I won't mind if it's born on the plane; give it something to talk about for the rest of its life!'

Quite unexpectedly, Seeta felt a smarting behind her eyes. Sheila reached out to her across her swollen belly in a sort of a half-hug, and said, 'So bye, honey, it's been great knowing you. Keep in touch...' And before Seeta could think of one word to say, she rushed out, back into the waiting lift and was gone, whisked down and away.

Seeta abandoned her walk, worried; wondered what the trouble was, said a prayer to Ganesh for a boy to be born to Sheila. She could not settle down to housework. Her heart was not in cooking. She put too much salt in the bisibela and none in the sambar. Narain came home, lost his temper at her vague and irritating unrest and pushing away the unpalatable food, yelled,

'What's the matter with you?' Hesitating because she knew how unsympathetic he had been to her friendship with Sheila, she said, 'Sheila has gone home. It seems Jake is in some sort of trouble...' Narain was not interested. Even before she had gathered up the plates he was on the phone to Graham.

That night when she lay listless in his grasp, he said roughly, 'Are you still worrying about that bint? Look, they got what they deserved. Someone was bound to blow the whistle on that scam. I bet they knew the score; that's why they could manage to get out so fast!' And he turned over and went to sleep, leaving Seeta wide awake.

Never before had she had trouble knowing right from wrong; there had always been someone to tell her: parents, teachers, uncles, aunts, in-laws. She felt lost not only because nobody was here to tell her, but also because she knew they would agree with Narain. And was that enough? Yes, Jake had done something wrong. Surely, Sheila had known what he was up to. As a result of all that she had let fall into his ear about her conversations with Sheila, Narain had somehow engineered Jake's troubles. And he and Graham intended to benefit from them.

But should *she* not decline to benefit from them? Was it not wrong to benefit from your friends' troubles, however deserved? Especially if you were in part responsible for them? She knew her father and mother would think her a fool or worse. Had they not dinned into her head that after marriage a woman's first duty is to her husband? And hadn't she done well, however unwittingly, by helping him? What was it then, that made her so unhappy? Something quite abstract, as yet obscure but demanding nevertheless, to which she owed her duty first?

She suddenly pulled up short, almost stumbling over the street sweeper who was standing, leaning on the handle of his broom, staring at a welter of scarlet petals which had fallen from the huge old *delonix regia* overhead. He was not making the least effort to sweep them away. Sadly she thought, Sheila had not succeeded in getting him to notice her, no matter which language she spoke. Impulsively she stopped and stood over him until he twisted his misshapen body upwards and glared at her. Hurriedly she said, 'Good morning.' He still glared at her through his small, red, almost-shut eyes and finally muttered something. Wonder of wonders, she thought, he said 'Good morning' to me!

It was fortunate she did not know Cantonese.

Hello, Stranger!

HIS wife was in there having their baby. He should have been inside to witness this unique and wonderful event, but he had explained to her when the subject came up that he could not face her suffering with equanimity. She rather valued his tender and easily-bruised heart and did not insist on his attendance at the birth. He had, after all, done all the other things: become tearful and thrilled when the news was broken to him, nurtured her through morning sickness, even made love to her in spite of her swollen figure and sore breasts. What's more, he had done them all willingly, delicately and efficiently.

So invariably did he do what she wanted, she quite often forgot he had been grafted onto her culture after he was all grown up. She congratulated herself on making him over in most ways. On the whole, she thought, it was better not to insist on his witnessing the birth. Truth to tell, she was afraid he might faint in front of the gynaec and the nurses!

So she was in there and he was sitting outside in the waiting room, listlessly flicking the pages of magazines. He was determined not to stride up and down like a caged animal as he had seen some fathers do in movies; so he just sat there waiting for his baby to be born and saying to himself, When the baby is born, I had better call Mother first and then Mani and Mohan.

He remembered going to see his mother when she had had Mohan. He must have been eight. There was a long green hall painted an even sicklier shade up to shoulder level in shiny oil paint. It was crammed with rows of iron cots for new mothers. Each cot had an iron crib next to it and a couple of folding chairs which were unnecessary since visitors had made themselves at home on the cots or on the floor. There were hardly any men, and those that were there, wore the same look of shamefaced superfluity as the empty chairs. His father, standing as far away from his wife and baby as the next bed-and-crib would allow, had asked if everything was all right, to which superfluous inquiry, his mother had not bothered to reply. But his aunt, the obligatory, attendant female relative, had said, 'All right?

After what she went through! I won't be surprised if there is no milk this time, and let me tell you, you had better stop this nonsense now.'

His father, looking more shamefaced, had moved uneasily in the direction of the crib. He himself had not been particularly interested in seeing the squalling and smelly thing in the crib and would rather have been out on the street playing, but thought he might as well see what it was that had taken his mother away from him for so long and so inexplicably and made her look so ill and exhausted. So he too, had crept up behind his father and had cast an equally cursory glance at his brother before being shooed out of what was rightly regarded as a female preserve.

This memory, so surprisingly clear when he had thought it irrevocably lost, made him acutely uncomfortable in this cozy and warm room with its carpet and fresh-cut flowers and framed prints and armchairs. He shifted in his chair and thought about his mother. A strange woman, he now felt; though during the time when he lived in her house, as man and boy, he had never thought about her at all one way or another, except to keep out of her reach on her bad days. A woman who repelled love and yet, demanded the overt manifestation of filial feelings which tradition decreed must be present in all sons: obedience, duty, gratitude and repayment for having brought him into the world and brought him up.

Guiltily he thought, he preferred the American way. You liked Mom and Dad well enough, did things with them when you were a kid. Then you grew up and had friends of your own and things to do when they became a bit of a pain. Then you really grew up and moved further away, left home. Finally everything came down to the once-or-twice-a-year Christmas or Thanksgiving visits, until you had kids. For their sake you visited a little oftener but soon the kids too got bored with grandparents and then the old folk were relegated to a chore, part of a past you didn't care to go over too often. You assumed they were okay until the summons to the deathbed.

But in spite of the generally admirable tendency here of everyone leading their own lives, his wife had summoned her mother now to be present at her side, and he was glad of that, because he could not quite get rid of the notion, ingrained in him through generations and centuries, that children were a woman's business. Deep down he found it difficult to picture himself as a true-blue American Dad. He saw rough patches ahead and sighed. He hoped he would have a daughter. On the whole, he thought, daughters demanded less from their parents. Mani, his own sister, had a perfectly workable relationship with his parents while he and his brother, especially he, suffered guilt and mortification in silence:

unspoken, unacknowledged, bottled-up feelings, emotions and silences that had led him down a terrible path.

He remembered the time he was in therapy. It had seemed as though the black cloud that had settled over him would never lift. Oh, he had suffered, contemplating everything from suicide to a precipitate departure for 'home'.

He suspected that he was a gloomy sort of a person to start with, not sunny and full of the goodness of life like his wife. That was what had first attracted him to her. She seemed to brim with optimism and good thoughts. He did grasp that a woman who was a stranger to life's wants, material, social, emotional or political, was more likely to be sunny-tempered than not. Still he thought it an attribute especially American: innocent, trusting and accepting. It was only when he got to know her much better—as well as he was ever likely to, he thought—that the nuances of her disapproval became discernible to him. He came to see that in spite of a general lack of friction in the marriage, his 'foreignness' was never understood or accepted; it was merely tolerated, at times corrected. A few exotic traits might have been allowed to be exhibited on appropriate occasions, but alas, he was not an exotic person—few urban, educated Indians are—and whereas she might have forgiven a large and exhibitable exoticism, his small and innocent solecisms galled her: turning off a ball game or turning down a barbecue. He had learnt to put up with ball games by now of course, but he still could not bring himself to eat fresh meat roasted in front of his eyes and filling his nostrils with its meaty smell.

He uneasily wondered how he would fare in the ball game or even barbecue department if the baby were a son. The only game he really knew how to play was gulli-danda. Last Christmas he had made and given a gulli-danda set to his nephew, just like the one he had given long ago to Mohan, the boy's father. They had spent hours of their childhood happily playing that game. His brother's wife had thrown away the two whittled pieces of wood. Thank God I am not married to *her*, he thought. He wondered if his wife would object to his making a set for his about-to-be-born child. He thought not. But then, why bother? He/she would be better off playing baseball with all the other kids. And the baseball paraphernalia would make a handsome Christmas gift too.

Actually, none of the things he remembered playing with as a boy would make an acceptable gift, let alone a handsome one: pieces of wood, stones and pebbles, little glass balls out of broken soda water bottles, discarded inner tubes and worn tyres, pieces of rope, a stout slingshot made from a Y-shaped guava twig, rubber bands, toffee-and-cigarette papers... He remembered with a smile the delightful games he and his friends had made up with these seemingly unlikely materials. Even cricket, that aristocrat of ball games, had been within their reach when they could rustle up between them a flat piece of plank, a lump of mud wrapped in rubber bands or inner tube, a bit of charcoal to draw the stumps on a handy, low parapet, and a comparatively tiny, open patch of ground.

He had become strong and hardy enough without ever having owned any bats and balls and racquets and dumbbells and shoes and exercise bikes. He had never owned even a pair of swimming trunks before he'd come to this land of plenty, and yet he could outswim almost everybody he knew here, with his ungainly crawl-cum-dog-paddle. He had learnt this stroke when his father had simply thrown him, at age five, in the well behind his grandmother's house. This was considered enough parental guidance in teaching a son to swim, and he had gasped and spluttered and struck out in that special stroke of his and survived. Later on he had happily jumped into any handy body of water, stark naked or clad in his underpants.

He smiled to think what his wife's reaction would be were he to try this method of coaching their child to swim. He supposed he would have to pay for the swimming classes and the tennis classes and the karate or judo classes and the French, music or ballet classes, the aerobic dance classes. And he, who had never learnt anything in classes except English and arithmetic and logarithms and chemical formulae and strength of materials and, of course, the long lists of Mughal emperors and viceroys of India, was capable of outrunning and outswimming all the men his age, who regularly 'worked out at the gym'.

As Mohan more than once said, after losing to him in the obligatory snow-run before the heavy Christmas dinner, 'Honourable Elder Brother (his ironic translation of Dada) was always a fast runner. He jolly well had to be, to keep out of the reach of Mother's rolling pin.'

His wife thought it a good joke, and he never disillusioned her because she would have been horrified to know that it was the truth; and getting a bit beat-up, boxed on the ear, hit over the head, or spanked on the bottom were no great things. He remembered well enough the times he had not run fast enough to escape the various blunt instruments aimed at him by parents, grandparents, teachers, uncles, aunts, cousins and older boys at school. Sometimes the pebble from the slingshot or the makeshift cricket ball missed its mark and went through a window and then neighbours joined in the chastising. A few knocks were what you were brought up to expect from life and quite a few of them were what you got. As you grew up, you learnt to give a few as well.

He could imagine the faces of his wife and her family were he to dilate upon this theme and conclude that none of it ever did anybody any real harm. It was unthinkable, of course, that he would ever hit his kids, but he would have liked to tell them how he was cuffed and spanked and how it never made any difference one way or the other. But he was afraid that if he said anything of the sort, instead of having a good laugh at the picture of Dad bending over with his pants down, they would think their grandparents monsters.

He sighed again. Was he likely to have any good laughs with this child? How did you communicate with someone who would know nothing of what your childhood, your boyhood had been like? What's more, who probably wouldn't even want to know? Who would, in fact, rather not know? How could a boy who got a whole ball game as a Christmas present ever know what it was like to fashion your own toys out of pieces of wood? What could a father say to a child brought up on games and music and jokes and food which had nothing to do with what he himself had loved and breathed and lived? Would Lata Mangeshkar mean anything to it? Would a meal of rice and dal with salt satisfy a hunger bred on hamburgers and pizzas and ice creams and colas and candy? What to him was simply 'food' was here 'ethnic' food or 'exotic' food, or worse, 'health' food. His child would never think of it as everyday, matter-of-fact food; and it would certainly think its father's preference for vegetarian food a kink.

For a moment he felt unbearably depressed. Like he used to. Like the times when he did not want to get out of bed, when he spent days and weeks, just going to the bathroom, eating boxes of cereal and going back to bed. Somewhere along the way though, he had found the courage, the resolution, the energy to get up and go to the psychiatrist. It had taken a lot of courage because he had been conditioned to think that only 'mad' people went to such places. He remembered slightly wonky people at home— an old aunt, a second cousin, a neighbour—who were swallowed up by grey-stone-walled, barbed-wire-surrounded, padlock-gated and dreaded government institutions for the mentally ill at Thana or Yerawda; institutions which never seemed to let out anyone they took in.

He had been afraid that he might disappear in a similar way. But he had found it in himself at last to seek help. For he had been so desperately unhappy, so alone; alone in spite of having his whole family nearby, his family whom he had helped emigrate. He did not want to beg them for help and they did not want to come forth to associate with 'a crazy', who might endanger their own chances of getting that coveted citizenship.

He did not really blame them. He knew the bleakness and the poverty of their lives at home and he could not find it in his heart to condemn them if they felt afraid that their escape from that world would be blocked by his illness, and if they therefore refused to gather around him in his distress. But he did feel that if all this had happened at home, they would not have thus abandoned him. At home, even those characters who had vanished into the mental institutions had not been abandoned; they had been visited, given clothes, sweets and pickles, talked about and worried over. Sometimes ward boys had been bribed (almost everybody is bribable in an institution of that sort) to allow some of the more harmless ones to leave the place clandestinely to attend some family festival. They were not shunned and obliterated, as he had been when he'd had the 'breakdown'.

There was something about the air here maybe, which brought out the selfishness that overrode millennia of tradition. And yet it was here that he had found a sympathetic and patient ear which had helped him to come to terms with the dichotomies in his soul. And it was here at last, that he had found love. Yes, whatever definition you gave to that word and that feeling, it was beyond doubt that it was the word he must use to describe what he felt for his wife. Honesty compelled him to admit at times that a big dollop of gratitude was mixed in his love, but it was love nevertheless.

He understood and accepted that she was not capable or perhaps even desirous of knowing what he was all about; just as he was not capable of understanding her. And he knew also that she would not sympathize with, acknowledge, or even be aware of the deep division in his being. But then, had he not left understanding and sympathy and all that behind when he set out for these shores? That was the choice he had made. And did he not, in return, have a comfortable and affluent life, a reasonably compatible wife, the satisfaction of having fulfilled his duties and obligations to all his family? And now, there was this child.

He must have dozed off, because he came to with a start as the door opened. It was his mother-in-law. He scrambled to his feet and rushed to her. She tilted her head to be kissed and said, 'Congratulations dear, it's a boy!' Still feeling awkward, after all these years, about these slightly formal intimacies, he kissed her cheek and said, 'Thank you, Mom, can I go see them now?'

'Sure! You go on in, dear.'

And he burst through the door at a run. His wife looked radiant, beautiful; exactly as new mothers are supposed to look. He dropped to her side and held her in a sort of a half-embrace and kissed her wherever he could, while she laughed at him a little, and said, 'What a beautiful little boy we have got, my darling!' and sent him off to see the baby. So he went into the nursery, gowned and masked, and was given his son to hold.

And at the touch of the little body, he felt an enormous wrench. This was it, he knew. This was the final, irrevocable step. He had to give up all those vague dreams now, all those strange and amorphous shapes that loomed around midnight, the dream-shapes of all his old and lost friends, of the streets of his hometown, the bare hills surrounding it, the row of small and poor houses in the raw new housing development where he and his team had broken so many windows with their cricket ball. He smelt again the hot summers, the mangoes ripening, the jasmines blooming; tasted again the eye-watering curry his grandmother used to serve with leftover rice; felt again the drying and filthy river-mud oozing and squelching under his naked body... This was it, then. This was goodbye.

This child, this son of mine, would never know what it was to want, what it was to play happily with two pieces of wood, what it was to fight his own brothers and sisters for a greater share of the food, what it was to hide the holes in his shirt with his fist, what it was to wear nothing but a succession of worn and too-large-or-too-small hand-me-downs, what it was to call at least a dozen women 'aunt' and just as many more 'grandmother' and be treated with affection and generosity in a dozen houses by people on whom he had no claim of any sort except that of innate hospitality, and finally, what it was to face sorrow and loneliness and rejection and humiliation in an alien country. This son, who would forever be an alien to the father as the father was an alien to these shores, this son was the final goodbye and the first link.

As the huge mass of that terrible, slatternly, grasping, unattainable subcontinent—parched in summer heat, bathed in glorious rain, frosted with winter winds, mistress of his hopeless love—crushed his heart like a plum in its fist, he looked at the dark and beautiful son who would live happily under the sun without ever knowing anything of this dark burden of his father's. And he said, softly, his eyes smarting with tears, 'Hello, Stranger!'

A Harmless Girl

FOR some reason best known to themselves, my large, popular and handsome parents decided to bring up their children to be innocuous and unobtrusive. As we were all at least as large, though perhaps not as popular and handsome, it took an enormous amount of parental direction to make us self-effacing. I can bear witness to the fact that they were not spectacularly successful where my brothers and sister were concerned, but by the time I came around, the last of the quartet, the enforcement and vigilance cadre had been augmented by three and I heard nothing throughout my childhood and teens except how I should make much less noise, how I should not put on (or out) the light because someone wanted to sleep (or read), how I should ask everyone else before I finished all the dessert, how my heavy tread disturbed persons of delicate sensibilities (my mother) or persons engaged in higher studies (my second brother), how I could not bring my friends home because people were practising the harmonica (my eldest brother) or people were going to give birth to babies (my sister), how I could not go to my friends' houses either because then I would be a bother to *their* mothers, fathers, brothers and sisters, how I could not ask my neighbours for a loan of their bikes to go to the shops because that might inconvenience them if out of politeness they could not say no and yet how I must never say no to loaning any of my precious possessions because that would be selfishness, and how I could not think of marrying my young hero because it would be very bothersome to his poor old widowed mother who did not approve of me at all. Even the horror of breaking china was based not on the loss of the broken item but upon the noise it made in breaking and the bother it would be to pick up the pieces. I suppose if I were about to die I would have been dissuaded on account of its being a great bother at that moment to everyone.

I grew up to be practically non-existent. In my eternal endeavour to live harmlessly, botherlessly and noïselessly, I learnt to tiptoe, to wear only flat, rubber-soled shoes, to eat and drink not only without making the smallest noise but even without making the smallest movement. My voice sank to the point of inaudibility and I learnt to sleep under any circumstances, even standing up. If ever I went in for my bath without a towel through dire oversight, instead of just shouting for it, I put on my clothes while still wet. Of course, I couldn't stand there dripping dry because someone else might want to use the bathroom just then.

There wasn't much I could do about becoming any smaller but I tried to be as thin as I could. This too had to be done unobtrusively because just as it was a great nuisance (to my brothers) for me to be greedy, it was a great inconvenience (to the cook or my mother) for me to be on diets. Also I had to remember to be healthy because it would be a lot of trouble to nurse me in sickness and it would be very inconsiderate of me to be undernourished and so a prey to infections which I could pass on to others. For a long time I did not know that the story of the little boy who, upon being asked his name, answered 'Johnny Don't', was supposed to be a joke. I might have answered, 'Hush Dear', or 'Don't Dear'; there wasn't much to choose on grounds of frequency of usage. In fact, as *obiter dictum*, 'Must You Dear' was also in the running.

I found myself going to bizarre lengths to escape the stigma of 'having made a noise'. When in my late teens, I was sometimes taken to the movies by a boy who would buy me a packet of crisps in a fit of extravagance, I would either try to swallow it whole in the intermission in my frantic hurry to finish it before the lights dimmed, or, if caught with it half-finished after the crucial moment, I would slowly and painfully render each crisp soggy under my tongue before noiselessly swallowing it. The problem of the packet making a noise as I fished in it was overcome by emptying the lot in my lap. One particular boy was so struck by this performance that he ended up taking me to *three* movies just to watch my antics with the crisps. I, in turn, was amazed by the intrepidity of the folk around me who munched and crunched and whispered and even laughed. I used to glance around nervously before noiselessly laughing even at a Pink Panther movie. I was also very good at noiselessly sneezing, coughing and, if the occasion arose, crying. Things like yawning, snoring, burping or farting were of course out of the question, and I would stop breathing until I was falling down in a faint if I got the hiccoughs.

And though, through this extremely unobtrusive and harmless behaviour, I ought really to have escaped all notice, I ended up inexplicably being the most popular person in orbit around the sun. I was the beloved pet of teachers, the favourite guest of hosts, the sought-after sister of siblings, the ideal employee of employers, the treasured friend of neighbours. 'Oh, she is marvellous,' they would all say. 'Never any bother to anybody!' I began to believe happily that that would be my epitaph if anyone noticed that my silence was due to death and not to my usual desire Not To Make A Noise.

Naturally, after waiting a long time to make sure that it was not going to be a bother to anyone, I noiselessly fell in love at a ripe old age, with the noisiest, brashest, heartiest, laughingest man anyone had ever met. No one had ever seen his mouth closed, not even in sleep, because then he kept it open and snored. He crunched, munched, roared and commented his way through every movie and naturally didn't hear a word of the dialogue. He began to laugh the moment someone began with 'And have you heard the one about...?' He thought that sneezing, coughing and all the rest of it were natural blessings to be enjoyed at their fullest and noisiest. If you didn't know that it was only one man coming up the stairs, you would have bet he was a herd of buffalo. In his enthusiasm for singing he had been known to shatter not only eardrums but also glass. Even so normally noiseless an action as writing a cheque could become an orchestration of percussion in his hands as he dotted the i's and crossed the t's, and tore off the offending member away from its fellows at the perforated line. He would put a full stop to this performance by throwing down the pen, which would fall off the desk with a brisk rattle. Then, dumping the chequebook in with the sound of a diver hitting water in a mis-dive, he would thunderously shut the drawer. For a more virtuoso bit, he would close it on his fingers and yelp like a stepped-on cat for half an hour.

Contrary to all my expectations, he was very popular too. People forever said things to him like, 'Oh, shut up, Hari,' or 'Watch out, you elephant,' or 'Ugh! How can you, you oaf!' or 'Are those the feet that sank a thousand ships?' Or 'Hari, you can't possibly make a crunching noise while eating a banana!' or 'Is that your stomach Hari, or Thunder on the Right?' And he just laughed and roared his way into everybody's hearts and was the beloved darling of his friends and family. There's no accounting for tastes.

It is my firm belief that the two sets of friends and families decided to throw us together out of sheer malice and waited to see the result in the expectation of a good show. They were not disappointed. We got married and moved into my father's house which I had inherited; and that stronghold of noiselessness, impeccable etiquette, unfailing orderliness, geometrical decor, and unimpeachable good taste exploded like my reputation. It was lucky that it was a solid house and contained most of Hari's normal day-to-day racket within its walls; otherwise neighbours would have begun to call up the fire brigade with the dawn when he woke me up (that's figurative because I could hardly have said to have slept on Omaha Beach through D-day) with his good morning kisses which sounded like Orlikons attacking the Bismarck.

Fortunately, for all the tremendous sound effects, he was not a very big man and one of the sure-fire ways of subduing him was simply to smother him in my large embrace. He got quite the wrong idea about my passionate nature on account of the frequency of this occurrence. As it was not possible at all times to execute this manoeuvre, I worked up many strategies to counteract what I saw as serious breaches of the Code of Silence. I sneakily laid down carpets on all surfaces, I instituted the use of plastics as opposed to metal and glass, I moved our sleeping quarters to the floor (saying it was good for our backs), I got rid of as much furniture as I reasonably (and sometimes unreasonably) could, I let the upper floor and walled up the staircase, I soundproofed the bathrooms. Still, the noise-level in our house at all times when he was at home was barely tolerable. And then he would burst into the kitchen (where I would be cooking noiselessly) from the living room (from where I could chart his unseen but very audible progress for the last five minutes) and say, 'Hey! Let's have some music and laughter in here, sounds like a bloody morgue!' and call up a brigade of friends to come and rattle up the place a bit.

Though in self-defence I learnt to be a bit more audible, there were definite limits to how much I could obtrude on people's attention. For instance, after exposure to Hari, I could actually take a swallow from a glass of water instead of sipping at it for fifteen minutes as I used to do, but I still shrivelled up in shame when, in a crowded restaurant, he would shove back his chair roughly, stretch out his legs under the table so he kicked me across it and say to the peaceable couple at the next table who seemed to be in the way of his expansive gestures (and who did rather look like they were listening to him hold forth), 'Hey, pull your horns in a little, a guy's gotta make a point with his hands, hasn't he? Why don't you join us?'. And to my astonishment, more often than not, they did join us for coffee.

Don't get me wrong. I am not cribbing. I loved the man, and like all loves that arrive late, I loved him with a love that was all-absorbing, encompassing and delightful. It was just that he was such a mystery; so entirely different as to belong to another species. I simply could not see any reason for him to be the way he was. He had a perfectly normal set of parents who must have said 'hush' and 'don't' to him; he had an elder brother who must have practised the harmonica or undertaken higher studies; he even had a sister who must have given birth to at least one child in their parents' home. I couldn't understand it, and finally I just gave up. He took to calling me 'She Who Must Not Be Heard' and people took to calling us 'The Odd Couple'. And then, much more sneakily than I had thought possible in him, he cooked my goose. I got pregnant.

Now, even in my limited experience, I had had quite enough to do with babies. I knew perfectly well that one cannot give birth to babies without any noise or bother, let alone bring them up to a reasonable age when one can begin saying 'hush' and 'don't' to them. To say that I was bereft of words is not to say anything, since I was generally always bereft of words. My total disruptedness could only be expressed in something totally alien to my nature. In a sort of a frenzy, I went out and got a whole large packet of crisps and sat down in front of the TV and deafeningly munched and crunched the whole lot under Hari's admiring ear as it were. He was also suitably gratified when I was noisily weepy, vociferously morning-sick, thunderously heavy-treaded. He was thrilled when I charged into whatever pieces of furniture remained in our home, rushed off to toilets in the middle of Mozart's symphonies, exasperated every friend and relative with finicky food-fetishes, made him run around at midnight trying to find exotic fruit for my cravings and snored much more loudly than him in the later months when my size made it mandatory for me to sleep on my back. All in all, the goddamn pregnancy was a revelation through which I discovered the delights of noise and joyously justified the necessity of Being a Bother.

At the end of it I gave birth, as noisily as I could, to a baby girl. I was relieved because I thought that it would be easier to make harmless, noiseless, unobtrusive people out of girls than boys and no empirical evidence had come my way to prove my thoughts wrong. However, right then, I heard some empirical evidence coming my way as that future inaudible and innocuous person gave a syringe-splitting scream. Fortunately, immediately after that, she was taken away into the bowels of the hospital to have things done to her that are done to newborn babies. When Hari came to see me, on what *he* thought were footfalls like feathers, he did sound like only one man and not a herd of buffalo. Maybe the thoughts of the onerous responsibilities of fatherhood were calming him down, or maybe the hushed and sepulchral atmosphere of the hospital, which was getting me down after nearly nine months of unbridled sound, was having a deadening effect on his feet. He kissed me quite soundlessly and asked in a whisper, 'Where is she?'

I stared at Hari. It was the first time I had heard him whisper and not heard him kiss. I said in my normal voice which had become quite audible by now, 'She is with the nurses. They'll bring her in a minute. And she is, well, she is audible at least.' He beamed noiselessly and I was again wonderstruck. He actually did not roar with laughter. Before I could remark upon this, the baby was brought in and handed to him. His beam widened. He blushed. He swelled. He almost shed tears. Yet he was quite mute and speechless. History was made.

And just then this little bundle of beauty and joy who was having such a pacific influence upon her father added to my empirical knowledge as I had feared from the very beginning. She opened her eyes and her mouth, took in a lungful of oxygen and let out that drip-bottle shattering scream. Hari and I, both quite horrified and quite simultaneously, said, 'Hush, sweetheart!'

Map

THIS is a map of my body.

I draw it anew, a half-century after my birth, because I find now, I hope not too late, that all along, the lineaments of the territory that I thought mine—contours, rivers, valleys, mountains, jungles, demarcations—had been drawn by another cartographer altogether, not me. And how did that happen? Well, I had never been particularly interested in my own geography and when a cartographer turned up, I trusted, welcomed him, because he—yes, unmistakably, he was a he—and his intentions appeared so scholarly, so objective, so *disinterested*. Plus he was a guest, and since it has been decreed for more than three thousand years that the guest, the stranger in our midst must be accorded the best welcome, he had it. And, let's face it, he was flattering. He delighted in me. His pleasure in treasures he found, hidden from my own senses, was unbounded. His relation to me was one of endless, ecstatic exploration. Another verb, close enough to that one comes to mind now, but did not then, not consciously. For was not exploration the reason I had let him in, after all? He had promised to make me known to myself. I was eager for this self-knowledge, hidden from me till then; thinking, if I don't know my own toes and fingers, how am I going to say I know myself? Not knowing, then, that to *be* myself could perhaps be enough. And he told me all sorts of wondrous things about me. How my feet were 'Grecian', how my hair a peculiar brown that shaded off into burnt umber, how my fingers each had a different face and a different character... Half the time I did not know what he was talking about, but I was sure it was flattering and therefore true. All the time his imagination was creating a me I did not know anything about.

I cannot say when I first had a fleeting suspicion that the me in his mind had nothing to do with the me in my mind, but now, now I find that he did, in the event, misunderstand, misrepresent and yes, betray a trusting fool—you betrayed me, you know—not unwittingly, but shamelessly, and even righteously. (I am doing this for *you*, my love!) All along, playfully, erotically, he worked on me—and I admit my complicity. Let us draw you thus; put this trench here, this fence here, this river is a natural boundary and so are these mountains; this is where we put the first line of defence—see these earthworks and cunningly hidden gun-turrets?—and in case that is breached— I don't seriously think it will be, but just in case, he said, let us have a bit of a jungle on the slope, brush and bush for ambush, and if that isn't enough—it's bound to be, he said, we'll surround the citadel with...with...tell me, what shall we surround it with? Thorns? Barbed wire? Man-eating tigers? And he laughed and I admit that I laughed too, thinking myself a man-eating tiger, no less, and planning to roll up his cartography in a tight ball and...but Marvell has been there before me.

And so according to his geological, geographical, military survey, we drew the lines on my body-map and fortified the places he said were vulnerable, taxed those he said were cultivable and usable—taxed reluctantly, he said, just as a small payment for his cartographical, cultivating, protective services—and waited; for fecundity, increase, yield... And there was much of that, and he got it all and the joy of it, and I became older and drier and fallower and of course I became crankier. Creaking in the joints and sick, always having headaches or the erratic periods of the climacteric, lazy if I could get away with it, taking refuge finally, in alcohol and dope, which was enough to breach any defences, however impenetrable. But, as days went by, I slowly began to wish and then work for his departure. For I actually began to ask: where was my delight in all this? Was I allowed to explore and know and map out his body? Fortify it and reserve it for my use and tax its terrain for my benefit? He pretended to be exhausted, working for me, but he seemed ok to me; just as eager and playful and gung-ho and turning his roving cartographer's eye to new body-maps. It was I who was worked out; so well-known now that I was of no more interest—not only to the cartographer, but to the cultivator, the sensualist, the voyager, adventurer...'

I was 'too much trouble' for him eventually. So, well, he said, that's it then, I'll be going, but don't you forget, you poor bitch, who drew your map and who fortified and protected and cultivated you. Mind you are properly grateful if and when I have need of your services, ok? I was stunned. Going? Just like that? I could hardly believe it. I wished my sickness were cured just like that, climacteric reversed, headaches gone, I again the young and beautiful, untrammelled maiden (I like to think I was that, but who knows?) I was before maps were drawn of me 'in order' to know and protect, cultivate, instruct, penetrate, fecundate me... But alas, no. Who can turn the clock back? I am what I am now.

I didn't really stir very much from my accustomed position on the couch as he left, for he had decreed that it would be best for cultivation, penetration and observation if I lay supine at all times, in the presence of outside predators like viruses and bacteria, or inside dysfunctions. After all, there were the defences he had constructed and there were the man-eating tigers, and there was he himself, if worse happened to come to worse. There was never any need to bother my pretty head about anything, was there? I watched him withdraw. He collected his paraphernalia, the cartographer's tools of the trade—his compasses, spirit levels, monoculars and binoculars, coloured pencils, rolls of paper... He cocked an eye at me regretfully, was going to say, 'It was nice knowing you,' but easily restrained himself, as was his habit, shrugged his shoulders and went.

I know I am nearly old, devoid of virtue (in the Chaucerian sense, meaning juice), mystery, treasure and adventure. But I am certainly not devoid of joy. It has not yet been pencilled out of me. I also know, happily, that no cartographer is likely to come my way now. I am master of my own territory at last. The rhetoric of trust and protection and cultivation is fading in my ears. So I was a fool, so what? That's nothing to be ashamed of. The world is thickly populated by fools. And I still have a good many good years in me in the company of all those futile increases you have left me; what with the occupation and interest in all their squabbles, their greed, their blindness...they distress me at times, but they help pass the time excitingly; sometimes, even constructively. Though I do at times think that I have got AIDS by now, or that the lives of my 'increase' have been blighted by various congenital or venereal diseases (those bacteria and viruses you so carefully tried to guard against while you encouraged cultivation, and perhaps also those internal dysfunctions?) or, who knows, by my addiction to opiates that I eventually took to, under your guidance, to blunt my increasing despair during the last years of our conjugation.

And so, now that you are gone—mercifully, regretfully, whatever—,I thought I would draw this map all over again. Get to know myself in a way I choose, redefine myself, re-imagine myself. Why not? I am my own cartographer now, and can imagine and draw what I please, in my own lineaments: Tibetan forehead, Terai-paddy hair, Himalayan breasts, Gangetic abdomen, Vindhya-Satpuda bush, Eastern and Western Ghat arms, Silent Valleys, Nilgiri legs, toes reaching out across bays, rivers of sweat running over all this and meeting unbounded seas over which I float like the Seshasai, or the whale, or a lump of mud, or a drift of seaweed, or any other material or creature in any 'myth of creation' not created yet, but will be, by and by, as I sit or lie down or sleep and think about it... Why not?

This is a map of me. These are my eyes. Bet you thought I am still going to say they are like obsidian or pearls or whatever, but they are just eyes. A bit short-sighted, and needing reading glasses too, but just eyes. These are my ears. They too, are not shell-like, or pointy-like-a-fox's, or long-and-gracefully-curved, but they hear pretty good. They heard the slam of the door as you left and then they heard some chopping, scurrying and scrambling as well—wonder what that was?—but they're ok. Then there're such things as breasts, almost useless now that I am either milked out or fallow; and at fifty they are certainly not pretty and I think I can safely dismantle those particular defences you put in there and the taxes you levied on their use. The stomach works well. Eat anything and live, that's my motto. You thought its rumbles disgusting, said the food made me stink, and of course wanted to control the intake, but that's just my stomach digesting things. Heh, heh, you should have waited a little longer; it would have chewed you up and shat you out and no one the wiser! Maybe it is not washboard-flat and muscular, but it's a serviceable stomach, and I am content. The legs and arms...a bit arthritic and creaky, (even with some prosthetic attachments since the amputations you insisted upon, for cosmetic reasons no doubt) but they work, they do what they are supposed to do. Even toes and fingers; they work, a few cracked ones included. You'll notice that I've left out all those valleys planted with thorn trees and bushes for ambushes and man-eating tigers. Well, now they are just valleys. Some uses still legit, some not. Some defences breached, some not. Some violated and laid waste, some cared for and lush.

It doesn't matter any more, does it? It's my body now and my map. I've even got names of my own to put everywhere. Not those 'naming of things' names you gave them, but names which I suspect I always had. For instance, this line of sweat is a river called Brahmaputra, maybe this is another river called Saraswati or Manusmara. Who but I can get her tongue around names like that? But *this* is the place where I live and its name cannot be pronounced by anyone who doesn't live here too. And this is what I eat and the names of things I eat are a mystery to all who do not eat them. You do not know the names of my body parts, you do not know where I live, what I eat, what I shit, what I conceive, give birth to, what I suckle... Your maps are all askew, cartographer.

And if you turn up one of these days, as you are bound to, in one disguise or another—are you a toymaker now? a cobbler? a medicine man, a jongleur?—you will not know me. Bewildered, you will say, what happened to this boundary I drew? And this river, what's its name? How come there's a road here where there were defence-works and a town or a lake where there were plains? You will try hard to see your old pencilled lines and signs, including those you had put up, saying, 'here be monsters'. You will not find them now. You will now enter *my* map of my body.

Welcome, stranger and guest, you, with one sandal missing (you told me that story once), unsuspecting king and conqueror, so clever at answering questions, you who did much for me and to me, a lot of it bad and perhaps some good. And alas, my dear, you thought you had cleverly done yourself nothing but good, and now find— do you?—that in order to live, to atone—do you want to?—or even not to atone, you have to blind yourself. Perhaps you do not see that, because you were always blind. Or, let's give you the benefit of the doubt, maybe you had had to blindfold yourself deliberately like Gandhari— you will not know her!—to justify whatever the consequences of your alchemical map-making. But now, if your eyes can be opened after all, and if you want any congress with me, you had better learn these new lineaments, this new cartography of my body which I have drawn up, dreamt up, and, most importantly, delineated with my language, and soon, because I am fast losing the ability to speak to you in that language of grateful submission which you coaxed, forced, struck from my throat.

This is the map of my body and these are the names of my body parts. I have imagined them all, all by myself, and so they are mine, above all.

(A tribute to Edward Said.)

Whatever Happened to...

A LOT of people see movies or TV with their eyes shut. They never even notice directors, producers, scriptwriters or supporting actors, let alone hairdressers and make-up men. But me, I am always watching for bit-players and bit-doers. Quite often, the 'bits' go on to become stars, and though then I lose interest, I continue to feel that I have somehow 'discovered' them as it were. I am the only person I know who has seen *Coma* three times only to catch Tom Selleck's bit in it. Also worthy of note are the main characters' aunts and nephews. Most folk remember Olympia Dukakis as Cher's mother in *Moonstruck* but who remembers her aunt? I do, that's who. I always win trivia games about trivial actors and itch to phone in the correct answer after some fool has 'er...er...'ed or 'oh...ah...'ed through his ten seconds on the 'whatever happened to' phone-in quizzes.

I told you all that to show how fascinated I am by the periphery of my life, by people who whizz past the corner of my eye as it were. Life in the corner of an eye can be quite entertaining, even when you are engrossed in whatever is in front of your face. It tantalizes, makes you think: If only I could take time out to turn my head, I might catch a whole host of new bit-players in the act before they become stars.

That's why I carefully file away people who have had the briefest brushes with my life. Supposing they become stars, I could write a book, at least an article, say: The P.M. as I Knew Him. In my file are people who sat next to me on a long journey, occupied the same corridor in an airport hotel, shopped briefly at the same supermarket in a small town in a strange country, went to nursery or primary school with me or were introduced by my husband as folk who were in school with him.

By and by, especially after this husband dumped me, I shed people who had known me as a young girl, a young woman, a young wife. There was no deliberation involved, they just dropped by the wayside. And yet off and on they did occupy my thoughts, their images as clear in the corner of my mind as they had been in the corner of my eye. I often wondered if they too were inveterate bit-player collectors like me and if I too occupied a corner of their thoughts from time to time.

Funny thing is, it was always the bit-players who made brief but recurrent appearances in my life. The star-billed hunks vanished for good, grand passions fizzled out; centre-stage, while I was standing on it, caved in; but the fringe guys stayed on. They assumed so reiterative a presence in my episodic and fragmented life because, I sometimes thought, perhaps I myself was about to be downgraded to a bit-role in it! More and more, I seemed to get lost in a dense, milling background of these minor characters scuttling in and out of the corners of my life. I was beginning to blend seamlessly into this clutter. Soon, no one would be able to tell me apart from it.

One morning the phone rang in Tokyo and when I picked it up, an unfamiliar voice said a name which belonged to one of those junior school, neighbour-in-some-city, shopper-in-the-same-mall sort of man. He asked me with becoming modesty if I remembered him. Indeed I did: he was the weedy-looking boy who used to sit at the front of the class putting his hand up for every question while I tied the girls' pigtails together and threw bread-pellets at the teacher from the last row. As time went by, he had made his scheduled one or two appearances in my life and I found that he didn't know quite all the answers though he still put up his hand. But mainly I remembered him because he was essentially the bit-player type: bit overweight, bit short on hair and looks, bit stuffy, bit worried about his children, bit afraid of his wife. And trying to make up for his shortcomings with a bit of humour. He was not born humorous, you see; just inspired by trendy TV serials where little bald guys get the girls because of a sense of humour and a 'warm and caring' nature.

When I went to see him in Tokyo as arranged, he looked so lost in the shining glitter of the Ginza, so ignored by the thick crowd flowing all around him, and so overwhelmingly glad to see me that I took pity on him and brought him home. He was impressed by my meagre store of Japanese phrases, my familiarity with Tokyo's underground system, my little rabbit hutch that I had furnished from the discards of Japan's affluent society and even by the fact that I had not put on as much weight as he had.

While working our way through a few beers, we caught up with a whole host of schoolmates, because what else was there to talk about? Between us we knew all about whatever happened to almost everybody who was in the class of '57 or thereabouts. The girls whose pigtails I used to tie together were happily married with a couple of children apiece. The boy who used to put cockroaches in our ink-wells was the chairman of his father-in-law's company. One boy and girl had married each other; another boy was a scientist in the Atomic Energy Commission; one or two had emigrated to the US and were teaching at topnotch universities; one girl had become a journalist; one had become a doctor, and so on. On the whole, a successful, happy and rich bunch. It seemed a bit miraculous to me, sitting so far from my little schoolroom and digging up all these hoarded gems from it.

And finally I said, 'And then there's you. A prosperous, executive-type globetrotter.'

And he laughed and said, 'Yes, and you of course. With your usual foresight, already in place in one of the most important countries in the world! How did you manage that, I wonder? You know, there's something I have always wanted to tell you.'

I know what you are thinking: I should have pricked up my ears and nipped *that* conversation in the bud right there! But upon this occasion you must understand the effect of loneliness in a stonewalling country like Japan, a few drinks more than I was accustomed to, a retreat into times when my life had a simple and straightforward direction, and the present feeling that I was being consigned to a bit-part in my own life, rapidly vanishing into the background, certainly as far as the class of '57 was concerned. So instead I said, 'What?'

And of course he launched into a long and sentimental speech about how he had worshipped me from afar for a long time. Apparently, he had always thought I was too attractive, glamorous, rebellious; therefore far beyond his reach. So he had never dared to approach me. This was so far beyond belief that I did not even bother to protest. I just gathered up the glasses and headed for the kitchen. He followed, ostensibly to help but actually to help himself to more beer and to continue the 'truth game', especially since both of us seemed to have decided to disregard the rule that there must be some truth in it.

To anyone as insecure as me, adoration, however false, secret and far back in the past is still welcome. And besides, he was a nice man, he meant well. Even if his once clear-cut features had become blurred with fat, his hair had decreased, and his alcohol consumption had increased alarmingly, he was still a nice man and he meant well. He was also an old peripheral in my life from way back when, and you cannot really mistrust anyone you have known for almost a lifetime, can you? Especially not if you are also guiltily aware of having brought the situation upon yourself by encouraging—or if not exactly encouraging, then by not actively discouraging—what could be termed mild advances.

I have always been acutely aware of having brought a lot of things, people and calamities upon myself. It's just as well that I have never been technically raped, because I am sure if I were, I would end up apologizing to the rapist for having been in the wrong place at the wrong time.

And yet I am not a fool. I knew I should get rid of him as fast as possible. But I did not see how I could do that without offending him. I certainly did not want to start a major drunken row in a quiet Japanese neighbourhood if my attempt at his precipitate eviction should backfire. I expected he would leave after dinner and so served it. But he continued to ignore it and make inroads into my beer supply. The firm but gentle farewell I had been practising in my mind never got a chance because by the time its turn came, he was in no shape to go anywhere. Knowing how difficult it would be to summon up my Japanese—in a reasonably advanced state of inebriation—to explain to the taxi driver how to take this drunken foreigner to his hotel, I spread the spare bed.

I am afraid the real reason was to find out if some not-so-secret proof of his long-standing and secret adoration was forthcoming. I had not only resigned myself to the inevitable encounter between futons, I had even begun to look forward to it. And so he held me and kissed me and drew me down beside him and partially undressed me and himself and continued to explore and caress me to quite an astonishing degree of excitement. When things did not seem to progress any further for quite a while, I decided to do a bit of exploring myself and was suddenly shocked quite sober to discover that he was completely unaroused. The poor, small thing lay practically undiscernible in the hairy pelt below his navel and there wasn't a spark of illumination in it.

I looked at his face and saw that he was not going to say anything very illuminating either and before I knew it, I had launched into apologies and excuses, saying how I was having an orgasm already and how being so close to him was all that I wanted anyway and how he must not mind and how I was sorry it wasn't as good for him... Lying awake later in my solitary bed, at last, it did occur to me to think but not say out loud that the bastard should have been apologizing to me.

Fortunately Tokyo is a bit out of the way. At least it seemed to be for the class of '57, and so it was some time before another such opportunity came my way to catch up on the activities of my favourite band of wandering bit-players. This time it was the girl who had become a journalist who called me up. She was very busy but could spare me a lunch at a local fast-food joint. Happily I got into a nicer-than-usual sari and a new pair of sandals and eagerly went forth. You might conclude that I am not the type who learns from experience.

I recognized her right away. The passing years had not made much difference. She was in jeans and a leather jacket, hung about with cameras and other journalistic paraphernalia, reading some sort of a press release. Confidence sat on her like a parrot on a pirate. She looked up when I said 'Hi', and did not recognize me for a moment and then laughed and said, 'Hi, is it really you? My God, you have changed. Surely you are only a few months older than me!' And I was instantly convinced of her truthfulness and sincerity just as I had been of the lack of veracity in my secret-but-now-revealed admirer. I am always convinced of the veracity of those who denigrate me.

She gaily proceeded to consume the lunch I bought her while chatting to me about whatshisname whom she met in San Francisco, and someoneortheother who happened to be on the same plane with her from Bangkok, and youknowwho who was covering the presidential inauguration in Washington, and... I sat there and took it all in, thrilled to bits to be brought up to date on the glamorous lives of my school buddies. Getting a word in edgeways, I eagerly asked, 'And did you tell them that you would be coming here and seeing me?' She gaped for a moment but caught herself up quickly and said, 'Of course. They were all amazed that you should have buried yourself in...I mean that you should live and work in such a, well, such an out of the way place, you know.'

I knew that they had done nothing of the sort. They had all forgotten me. Mechanically, I answered a few questions about shopping in Tokyo and the cheapest places to buy tape recorders, and let the conversation lapse. Then, in the lacuna, she remembered my previous enthusiasms and picking up what she thought was a more congenial theme, asked, 'And whatever happened to...?' Without waiting for her to finish, I said, 'I don't have the remotest!'

In the small silence that ensued, I imagined them all getting together somewhere in the world, going on a long nostalgia trip, and, after having remembered and laughed over even the peon who used to ring the end of each class on a big brass bell, one of them asking, 'And whatever happened to whatshername, you know, the peculiar girl who used to sit at the back...?', and this woman or my secret-admirer-and-non-lover answering, if they happened to be there, 'God alone knows. She just dropped out of sight, didn't she?'

I opened my mouth to apologize for the abrupt remark which had caused the hiatus in the conversation, but she hadn't noticed it and was already preparing to leave, gathering her stuff together. She said, getting up, 'Well, I must run; I have an appointment with the chairperson of the opposition party. It was good seeing you after all these years. I expect I will run into you again some time, some place; till then, goodbye. I will tell everyone you said hi.' And she left me with my mouth still open and the too-ready apology still unuttered. And don't ask me who played Third Murderer... I don't know.

Smile and Smile and...

THE Japanese face is not built for smiling. Its wide cheekbones, small eyes, narrow mouth, thick and tight skin do not scrunch up happily into brackets and crows' feet. Nor is the Japanese social convention conducive to expressions of bonhomie. It insists that on set occasions you stretch your back but not face. Wary contact with foreigners has revealed to the Japanese that 'others' smile to express goodwill, so now when they meet foreigners, they stretch their mouths into grimaces which still can't be called smiles by any stretch of imagination. In this endeavour to emulate some foreign ways, as for instance in their use of the English language, they are mistaken about intent, bizarre in execution and confident that they are on the right track.

While living and working in Japan, I had learnt to withhold wide smiles which my friendly nature normally pasted across my face at the slightest excuse; and had returned to my native land possibly minus a few wrinkles but probably with an incipient ulcer, hoping to be rid of the Japanese at last. So it came as a shock when, hardly a year later my boss decided to post me back there. Sensing my dismay, he said soothingly that it would only be for a few months. He was unhappy with the sales figures and wanted me to take charge of the Japanese office to show them how to co-ordinate properly with the head office.

When I began to tell him that it was impossible to 'co-ordinate' two such fundamentally incompatible outlooks as the Indian and the Japanese, he pointed to the plaque (strategically displayed on his desk, a present from his wife no doubt) which said, 'The Boss may be wrong, but he is still The Boss'. (Yes, he was that kind of a Boss, but he paid good money.) So, I swallowed my objections, obtained a visa, flexed my spine, dusted off songs I had hoped to have forgotten (more of this later) and prepared to go.

Even in my previous capacity as a junior employee, I had been a problem to Japanese colleagues. Since I was staff, I could not be dismissed like the giggling, tea-making, pencil-sharpening, plant-watering OL (office lady), but being a woman, I could not be included in their bar-hopping and karaoke-singing. They'd never had to deal with women as equals. Even their 'equal' women: doctors, lawyers, professors, councillors, 'knew their place', being Japanese. I refused to put up with being treated as anything but equal. (In fact even that was a concession to them as I am a firm believer in female supremacy). In the event, they found a typically Japanese solution: they simply decided to ignore my being a woman; and I ended up bar-hopping and karaoke-singing with them.

This last consists in tuneless braying of popular schmaltz to recorded music, and passes for serious entertainment under the influence (hence the aforementioned dusting off of old songs). However, they didn't take me along to porno movies and 'love hotels'. I didn't mind because Japanese porno didn't do anything for me, abounding as it did in soft-focus back views; or flowers, candle-flames, silk drapery and bonsai trees placed at strategic points; and though I could register in a 'love hotel' and go to sleep, I was sure they would be embarrassed at my presence there as they did not want me to be conversant with their peccadilloes. So at the end of the karaoke sessions I said goodnight, caught a taxi and went home.

But this time around, I was going to be an insurmountable problem to them since I was going there as Boss, though inferior in their eyes on account of being Indian and a woman. And I was going to enjoy rubbing their noses in it.

Fortunately, the Japanese are disinclined to create 'situations'. However bad they feel, they behave and work as required. Strikes, non-cooperation, working-to-rule, office-politicking and backbiting are Indian specialities, rarely served and consumed with as much relish anywhere else. As long as you correctly uttered the everyday 'things-to-say' in the correct tone of voice, respected and exactly followed the line of command, did not display a tendency to talk politics, economics, or sociology, never said anything worth listening to or replying to, you got along fine in Japan.

I was received correctly by the bowing, bland, courteous Mr. Miyura, erstwhile manager, now my second-in-command. And was immediately stonewalled by him into giving up any ideas about hiring a car and a flat; into approving an office plan which necessitated my facing the entire staff like their headmaster; and into letting him deal with Japanese customers while I 'co-ordinated' with Indian suppliers. Though I did not particularly object to most of his other 'suggestions', I knew I would have to join battle over the last as that was what my sojourn in the midst of the Heavenly Race was all about. Actually the seating plan worked in my favour as it allowed me to poke my nose into everyone's business which, being a true-blue Indian, I always considered my own. I also had another arrow up my sleeve: a working knowledge of Japanese.

All through the first weeks, I sat at my desk, keeping my eyes open, reading faxes, nodding at everything Mr.Miyura 'translated' for me. He was not one of the people who had previously worked with me. In fact I found that the entire staff in the office had changed in my absence, the turnover for such jobs and such small companies as ours being quite high. I soon realized that Miyura was certainly not dishonest; nor was he enthusiastically partisan. At times I even heard him agree—more in sorrow, you understand—with customers who turned down a shoddy bit of work in keeping with the strict quality control clauses we had had to write in for the Japanese buyers. Instead of promises of replacements, better goods, complaints (via me) to head office, there were cancellations of contracts. This seemed to be the root of the trouble. I was biding my time and awaiting the moment when my temper got the better of me.

One day a customer said, 'That's Indians for you!', and I heard Miyura sorrowfully agree. I lost my temper. Shoving my chair back I crossed the floor to his desk and leaning over him said with excessive politeness, and in English, hoping that the customer didn't understand it, but not really caring if he did, 'In that case, Mr. Miyura, you must be ashamed of working for us!' He was almost blasted out of his seat with shock. Colour flooded his face and receded, leaving it looking sick. I turned to the customer and asked him in over-correct, textbook-learnt, but comprehensible and serviceable Japanese what the trouble was.

It took him a while to realize that it was Japanese—which he knew was difficult, colloquial and impossible for foreigners to understand—that was issuing from my mouth; and even longer to grasp the fact—difficult and impossible for him to understand—that I was The Boss. Though I succeeded in eventually soothing him before sending him away, I was definitely aware that I had created a 'situation' in the office, thanks to my misplaced patriotism. Had Miyura not been Japanese, I would have stood him a drink, apologized for misleading him about my knowledge of his language, and would have directed him to refer all contractual matters to me. And he would have accepted my instructions or resigned, letting me find a more congenial manager.

However, being a Japanese male is tricky business. Perhaps they do feel superior, or perhaps they hide an inferiority complex under a show of superiority, whichever. But the myth of their superiority is nurtured by the whole society from day zero. In the interest of expediency, they might pretend to humbleness vis-à-vis some males among their conquerors, such as the President of the United States. They would not assume such a posture before the inferior races of the East; most certainly not vis-à-vis a female of that despised order. Miyura would be thinking of killing me or killing himself; actions, neither of which I was in favour of.

I wondered what to do next. Other staff realized only that I knew more Japanese than they had suspected, but Miyura sat palely at his desk like a thin Buddha, meditating upon his hands. By the time the customer left, I had not found a solution except to get him out of there. I spoke as casually as I could: 'Miyura-san, will you please take me to Kitano-cho to look at a flat on a short lease?' I wondered if he'd refuse, but of course he just followed me out. In his car, I said, 'I'll direct you,' and took him by a complicated route to a pretty monastery garden I remembered. When I asked him to stop there, he said colourlessly, 'You know this town well.'

'Yes, I do. I'm sorry I misled you about that too.'

'I wish you hadn't. There was no need.'

He seemed to be trying out a smile. I could not myself see now what the need had been, and said, not quite truthfully, but quite incoherently, 'Well...I didn't want to make you...I wasn't sent here to...it's not that we don't trust you...I don't mean to take away your...,' and stopped, because, after all, I *had* come here to see why he wasn't more aggressively successful, and I *did* mean to take a lot of responsibility and authority away from him.

He said with a more successful smile, 'But you're The Boss. I expect you to correct me when I'm wrong. I'm always willing to learn.'

'Then let me tell you right now that you shouldn't have agreed with Mr. Minami. Why did you ? You should be more aggressive...'

'I find it best not to argue with a dissatisfied customer.'

'But you lost his order.'

'No, no. I would have gone back with better samples when he felt less aggravated. I don't lose orders.'

'And why didn't *you* talk to me about all this strategy?'

'I thought you would soon see that, overall, I didn't lose us any business.'

I felt ashamed and said a little bitterly, 'Anyway, you should not be so eager to join in the criticism of Indians!'

'I'm sorry. I would not have put my customer-soothing agreement in such bald terms if I knew you could understand me.'

We were back where we started from but I was relieved that neither homicide nor suicide was on his priority list. After a small silence he asked, 'Shall we go back? Or do you really want to look at a flat near here?' I was surprised into a smile, which he competently returned and I said, 'We must have a drink in your favourite bar one of these days.'

We got along better after that. We even had a few drinks sometimes on the way home. He seemed even more private a person than most Japanese and never talked about himself. The only things I found out after our time together were his favourite karaoke songs and his preference for brandy. Mostly we talked about the inane things that people forced to be well-acquainted (but not desirous of getting to know each other well) talk about; and welcomed the diversions of alcohol and tuneless braying (he was in the Top Forty compared to me).

Though seemingly a regular, he was not on friendly terms with the others. When I remarked upon this, he said, smiling (he was making strides, this boy!), 'I don't come here that often without you.'

I was indignant. 'Do you think that exposing my tone-deafness is my preferred form of entertainment?'

He smiled more widely, and catching hold of the mike sang sentimentally about a dark-eyed lady, whereupon I pointed out that he must mean the entire female population of Japan, and he shook his head and continued smiling. He was really coming along in the smile department.

Then around Christmas, which Japan celebrates more fervently than any 'Christian' country I know, he asked for leave. This was so unprecedented an event in the annals of Japanese Commercial History that I goggled at him.

He smiled and said he had to go to Hiroshima. Hiroshima! In the dead of winter!

I could think of little else more dreary, and asked, 'What on earth for? I cannot spare you just now!'

His smile broadened and I discovered he could smile quite well after three months' exposure to me. He said, 'I'm glad to be indispensable, but I've business there.'

'Business?'

'Private, but truly important.'

Impulsively, and also intrigued by this private 'business', I said, 'You know, I have never been there. Shall I also come and see some of our customers?'

Smile in place he said, 'Why not? It's a nice city. I'll take you to eat *nabe*. Meet me at the Castle?'

Business over, I had a couple of hours in hand, and went to the Peace Park. A mistake. Ended up feeling hopeless and weary; willing to resign from the human race. Couldn't bear to look at another piece of commonplace yet devastating memorabilia, could not take in the statistics. Miyura came up as I stood by the river throwing in pebbles, head empty of thoughts but beginning to pound. He took one look and said, 'Peace Park'.

I nodded and hoped he was not going to begin on Poor Japan, The First Victim Of The

Bomb, but he just took my arm, and we were soon seated by a *hibachi* in a cozy restaurant, imbibing warm sake, engaged in the usual small talk. I told him I was astonished to find the city easy to browse in, pleasant and unhurried. I admitted shamefacedly that I had not visited it before because my first reaction to it had been horror.

He agreed it was pleasant, despite the associations, and now the industrialization, adding, 'I went to school here.' He smiled at my surprise as though born smiling, and said, 'I had a very undistinguished scholastic career!'

I suppose I should have expected it. Indian companies, however prosperous, cannot compete with Mitsubishi, Nissan or Nomura for graduates of Waseda, Tokyo and Kyoto. Politeness compelled me to say, 'But you speak English so well, I thought...'

He stopped topping up my sake-cup and said, still smiling, 'Oh, no. Never went to any of those great universities. Learnt English here, in the American orphanage. I am a *hibakusha*, you see, a Child of the Bomb. That's why I must report quickly to the hospital here, where I am registered, in case I notice any unusual symptoms.'

I found myself outside in the snow, being sick over leafless azaleas, and became aware of Miyura holding me, smiling apologetically, saying, 'I'm sorry, I didn't mean to make a secret of it, but I didn't...didn't want you to think I was some kind of a...you know how people...it's not that I don't trust you...I'm sorry.'

As he stopped, I said feebly, 'Don't *smile* when you say that, dammit!'

The Debt

WHEN Anita first met Sajan Singh, she had little information about India, and even less curiosity. She knew it only as a country that occupied a rather large area on the map of the world, was mentioned occasionally in newspapers for its floods and droughts, and was overpopulated by poor people. Never in her dreams had she thought that she would someday meet a man from that country, fall in love with him and actually end up marrying him. Yet that indeed was what had happened.

A girl from some obscure town in Texas, she had a chance to come to Berkeley thanks to her brains, and the very first day in her class she had come across Sajan, bearded and moustached, dark and foreign and dressed in strange clothes. She had been so taken aback by his strangeness that in the beginning she never thought about his personality. Later, she learned to ignore the strangeness of his turban, his dress, his hirsute face, and focus on the familiar: his fluency in English and his astounding scholarship. In fact he was the best student in her class of microbiology. Of course it helped that he was not given to talking about himself, that he preferred to stay in the background, that he was shy, reserved almost to the point of being mistaken for a misanthrope. The class was small. Although all of them were doing their own research, they would meet in the weekly seminars. The two came to know each other in course of time. At first their discussions were about their studies, the seminar topic, the professors, the other students; later they touched upon more personal matters.

Sometime in the second year Anita asked him about his home, his people. He told her very little: Mother died when he was young...three older sisters...father a doctor...home in a town north of Delhi...education all on scholarships... The tone of his reply was, 'what is there to tell, there are thousands like me in India; it's the same story as everyone else, more or less.' She had no curiosity about the matter anyway, so the subject was dropped for good. The third year of their friendship and the last year of her doctorate she sensed that she felt something more for him. She was confused. But she thought about it with the typical thoroughness of American girls. She the typical thoroughness of American girls. She measured the nature, length and strength of her feelings, asked herself whether it was wrong to feel that way. She discussed it with her parents, her close friends, some of her professors, and the counsellor of the university who was also a psychologist. When she realized that it was the genuine, noble feeling of true love, although the focus of it was a strange foreigner, she went straight to Sajan and told him, 'I love you.'

He didn't hug her with joy as she expected, but instead asked her with a smile, 'So what do you suggest I do about it?' For a moment she wondered whether it would be wiser to step back right then since he was asking such a question. But she had considered everything so thoroughly before coming to her decision, that she couldn't just give the matter up. So she said with all sincerity, 'People who fall in love usually marry each other, don't they?' The smile lingered on his face although she thought that she saw a trace of pity, a little sorrow in it. He only said, 'Is everything that easy here?' She did not understand the question. But apart from that, she did have a reasonably good understanding of his nature. He had been mostly brought up by his three elder sisters. Rarely did he see his father, the doctor. So he must have acquired a habit of giving in to the demands of women.

After his doctorate he got a job in the same university, and then at last, he did marry her. He mentioned to her that his father was dead opposed to his marriage, but the letter that he received was in Punjabi. She didn't ask him for details, and he didn't give her any. After that he never received any letters from India, so she gathered that his family must have disowned him. Good riddance, she thought. Now he doesn't have any excuse not to settle down right here. She was a little puzzled though. All her friends and her family were so liberal that they were ready to accept him in spite of his being a dark foreigner, in spite of his strange religion, turban, beard and all, and his people should disown the daughter-in-law who is well-educated, pretty, well-to-do, blond, and American! What strange pride!

Their married life started like everybody else's. She found a job in a hospital. Her parents gave them a small apartment as their wedding gift. He even shaved off his beard and moustache and gave up the turban at her insistence. In short, apart from the fact that Sajan was not, in fact, a true-blue American, they were quite like the average young American couple of their age. Sometimes she would sense his foreignness in some small matter, but she learned to ignore it. In fact, she was quite happy that compared with other American husbands, he was so much more courteous, so obedient, so willing to help in the house. He was still a little shy. When Sara or

Katie from the neighbourhood flirted a little at a party, he would blush and hide behind Anita.

She came to know how different he really was only when she became pregnant. She had no intention of having a baby. She was quite satisfied with her job and her research, and did not want to interrupt her career right then. It was by mistake that she had conceived, but she didn't make a great fuss about it. One day she casually mentioned it to him. For a moment Sajan's whole face lit up.

'Darling! How wonderful!' he said, getting up and gathering her in his arms. It must have been the first time he had spontaneously shown so much affection.

She pushed him away and said, 'I really don't want a baby you know, at least not right now. I have made an appointment at the hospital tomorrow.'

His face twisted in pain. He didn't want to understand what he had heard, so he asked, 'Appointment? What for?'

'To get rid of it, of course,' she said, rather brusquely. His eyes grew round. He said in an unusually loud voice, 'Anita, no! Never!' And then realizing that she had stiffened at that, added piteously, 'Please, please...'

When she saw all that entreaty, that begging on his face, she was startled. For a moment she thought it would have been easier had he thrown a tantrum. She turned to pick the coat off the hook, and going towards the door, said, 'Let's leave it. We'll talk about it later.'

But he came around and stopped her. For the first time she realized how big, how so very big he was, compared with her. She got really mad when she found she couldn't tear herself out of his hold. She remembered what she had once read somewhere: Indian men regard their wives as slaves and treat them as heir-producing machines.

She gave up her struggle and said in a tone of contempt, 'In your country they may think of women as just baby-making machines, but don't forget that I am an American. I don't want to live simply as a female animal, sacrificing my intellect, my personality. I will decide when to have a child if I decide to have a child at all. Understand?'

'How can you say that? Don't I have any right over this baby? Don't I have any share? Please Anita, have pity. Don't destroy our baby.'

'Stop being so melodramatic. Why say 'baby'? It's only a clump of few cells. I didn't think you were so old-fashioned, such a hidebound stick-in-the-mud.'

'What can I do to change your mind? I am begging you; shall I fall at your feet? Please grant me this, please!'

With every word of his, with every gesture she became more perplexed. She wondered how it was that although he was really so different, so strange, she had never noticed in all these five or six years. What she felt at the moment was a little dreary contempt for him. As he moved away from the door in his urgency, she quickly slipped through it and went away.

She never could understand or explain the malignancy of fate which decreed that that very day, the bus that Sajan took every day to go to work should meet with an accident and he should be critically injured. He lay in a coma for four weeks in the hospital and then became a statistic along with the others who had died in that accident. She didn't even know the address of his father to cable him the news, but the university office supplied her with it. By the time everything was over and she recovered from the deathwatch, the funeral, the shock, it was too late to terminate the pregnancy. What Sajan could not have achieved while living, he had achieved by dying, she thought in her bitterness.

There were many who showed sympathy but no one could understand the confusion in her mind compounded of sorrow, bitterness, and a dry, grey hopelessness as well. She shut up her apartment, took leave of absence and went to live with her mother. Life in that little, sleepy, small, monotonous town made her mind go numb. Every day would pass with the same blankness while she would swing back and forth on the porch swing. She could not think of what she was to do now, nor of what was to happen to her child. Finally, it was the child that brought her back to life. It kicked her from inside. It insisted that it was alive. That 'clump of cells' changed her body, it made her awkward, heavy, sick. Finally it made her aware of its existence in spite of her numbed mind. Although intellectually she had realized that that 'clump' was her baby and Sajan's, she only accepted it totally when the son was born and she saw that he looked exactly like Sajan. And she realized with a new, jolting certainty that there was no Sajan any longer. That was the first time she really felt like a widow, the first time she felt the pure pain of the unending loss of his nearness. That feeling had no bitterness in it, no grey dryness, just sorrow at the memory of Sajan. A deep sense of loss of all those qualities that were Sajan: his guilelessness, his gentleness, his shyness, and his intelligence.

When she talked to her parents about this, she realized that contrary to what she had earlier thought, nobody had really understood or accepted Sajan. In fact, although nobody said, 'good riddance', she could nevertheless detect a general sense of relief that he was no longer around.

And so, she quietly returned to her own house and work. She found a live-in help and resumed work. There was relief in work. But there was sorrow in watching how much the growing boy resembled his father. Once, while she was giving him a bath, she wondered why she had named him after her own father and not Sajan's. And on that thought she got up and searched the whole house and found Sajan's old passport and looked for his father's name: Bishambhar Singh. She could not really get her tongue around the unfamiliar mix of consonants and vowels. But she thought it sounded sweeter than the strange sound of her son's neither-here-nor-there name: Peter Robert Singh. On the first page of his passport was also an address. Who knows on what impulse she sat down to write a letter?

The letter never got written. The phone rang. It was her lawyer calling to tell her that the matter of compensation for the heirs of the victims of the accident was finally settled. She could come next week to the office of the bus company. A letter was on the way to that effect, but her lawyer had called first with the news. That check adorned with a lot of zeros scorched her fingers in the bus company's office. She thought, While living, I rated his value at nil, but dead, he is worth so much to this bus company! She kept the check in the drawer of her desk and didn't think about it for a while. But one day on her way to work, she took a detour and ended up at a travel agent's office. After a little hesitation, she asked him about India. He scattered colourful advertisements and brochures on the desk. In front of her bewildered gaze sparkled the Taj Mahal, The Gateway, The President's residence, village beauties, tribal dancers, Kashmiri houseboats, snow-covered peaks of the Himalayas, temples of Tirupati and Jagannath, Ajanta and Ellora.

With her Bankamericard she bought a ticket right away. It was the first time the agent had seen a customer wander into his office for a casual inquiry and go away with a ticket. He muttered something about it being quite warm there now and quickly rang up a few numbers to settle the matter. He took it upon himself to get her a visa and happily waved her goodbye.

Anita really felt the impact of her decision for the first time when she landed in Delhi. She was dead tired by the twenty-four hour long journey. Peter was screaming. She thought she had entered an oven. She was used to hot summers in Texas, but this was something else. Everywhere there was a sea of confusion, of noise, of people. Some dressed in suits and some that looked just the way Sajan did at first. There were air hostesses and other pretty women in saris, hippies in jeans and tunics, youngsters in mod clothes, it looked like a carnival. She wondered why everyone was shouting all at once.

The baggage conveyer had broken down, so her bags came in after two hours. Peter had cried himself to sleep. She held him somehow with one arm, shifting from foot to foot. If she could, right then and there she would have jumped onto a plane that would take her back. When finally her suitcases did arrive, she dragged them one by one to the customs counter. But people pushed and shoved her and rushed ahead of her. When Peter got up and started screaming again, an officer spotted her and brought her to the front of the queue. She had nothing to declare except Peter's clothes and hers, so she was let out at once, and when she came out, she just stood there petrified. She had just upped and left, and now she did not know where she was to stay, what she was to eat, or drink, or who to approach in need. Nor did she know how to get to Sajan's father. She simply stared in front of her, and rocking Peter, stood near her suitcases. A hippie came to ask her where she was going. She checked the address in the diary from her purse. Roorkee. He shrugged his shoulders, said, 'I don't know. Ask the cop. Do you have any money on you?' Anita shook her head. The hippie finally took pity on her and led her to the policeman, but he could not understand her, so he took her to a table where a sign said, 'May I help you?'

The attendant at that desk advised her that the best thing would be to stay in a hotel overnight and go to Roorkee by taxi next morning. Without asking her permission, he rang up and booked her a room in a hotel. By the time she came back for her baggage, the suitcase with her clothes in it was missing. She felt so desperate, she even forgot to weep. Again the policeman. He still couldn't understand. Again the interpreter. Some documents were made, some signatures were necessary. An address was given where she could purchase a few clothes. Finally when the taxi brought her into the air-conditioned coolness of the five-star hotel, she felt the tension snap and tears flow. Poor Peter at last lay silent in the cool darkness of the room. His skin was already raw with prickly heat. 'At least this hotel is like any other American hotel,' she said with a sigh of relief and, after a shower, dropped into bed.

When she resumed her journey the next day, she felt that the nightmare had also resumed afresh. There was the larger oven outside and the smaller inner oven of the old taxi in which six people were stuffed to be baked and roasted. Everyone was sweating and gasping. It was as if they were incapable of doing anything else in this heat. The parched, dusty soil, dried up, leafless trees, skin-and-bone cattle, dark, stunted people, here and there a man looking like Sajan, tall and turbaned; everything passed unheeded before her hot and tired eyes. Peter was shrivelled up from the heat. He was not screaming any more, just whimpering. When Anita's mind started to revert to numbness as an escape from the horrible reality, she made a strenuous effort to shake it alive, and asked the man sitting next to her who was sticky, sweaty and smelly, 'Are you going to Roorkee?' He just grunted. She asked again, 'Do you know Doctor Bishambhar Singh in Roorkee?' He only stared at her. As it was, he had shrunk as much as he could so that he didn't have to sit jammed up against a strange woman, a foreigner at that. Yet, whenever the man on the other side pushed him, he would fall against her and apologetically try to move as far away as he could.

Anita was not much surprised to see six people stuffed in so small a car. She had seen the ocean of people everywhere around her, and could understand the shortage of space. But she had become wiser after paying an exorbitant bill for just one night's stay in the hotel that morning, and had inquired first the fare before getting into the taxi. Thirty rupees each. She saw that the driver charged the same fare to everyone. She thought it reasonable, and so had got in.

On the way she was dismayed to see only dusty, sun-parched industrial towns lining the road, with shabby, crummy little shops, dry, steaming hot lanes, and mud-brown houses with a lost, forgotten, godforsaken look. Where was that dream world of the Taj, snow-clad peaks, the swaying coconut palms, colourful village beauties? She began to think that perhaps the grand fountains, the broad roads, the tall buildings with air-conditioned rooms and gardens full of flowering trees and lush green lawns that she had left behind in Delhi had been a mirage in this desert. While crossing the bridge on the Jamuna, the driver had turned back and said for her benefit: 'Jamuna river.' But since she did not know what Jamuna was, nor why one should be curious about it, the information was wasted on her. All she felt at the sight of the small trickle of water in the middle of a broad, sandy bed was a little contempt.

When the taxi stopped at some place and people got down, she thought she had reached her destination and started getting her suitcases out, but the driver said, 'No no. Meerut. Tea.' God knew how they were drinking the steaming hot tea in this terrible heat. After drinking tea, of course, they all began to perspire more freely. The man who had sat next to Anita offered his seat to the gentleman next to him, perhaps thinking, If this woman starts to talk to me after just an hour's journey, heaven knows what she might get up to after three! The other gentleman was not ready to give up his seat next to the window, but after a little persuasion, he came and sat next to Anita. Quickly he took out a piece of candy from his pocket and offered it to Peter. 'Sweet baby! Take sweet!' Peter resumed his crying at this overture by a total stranger. The gentleman shrank away hurriedly, saying, 'Sorry madam!' Anita embarrassed, said, 'He is a bit shy.' At that the gentleman broke into a lengthy speech about shy children and outgoing children. All his children and grandchildren apparently had no fear of strangers.

Then he asked, 'You are foreign, no?' Anita nodded. 'Where you are going?'

'To Roorkee.'

'You know someone there?'

'My father-in-law.'

'What name?'

'Doctor Bishambhar Singh.'

'Oh ho ho! So you are Doctor-sahib's daughter-in-law? Poor fellow, how many calamities can fall to one man's lot? Is this his grandson? Good, good. It seems you have come to look after him? At last now he might recover after seeing his grandson. And where is Doctor-sahib's son?'

Anita, staggering under the weight of all these questions, somehow managed to say, 'He died last year in an accident.'

'Are 're 're 're ! So that's why Doctor-sahib is so sick! What a fate! Even the promising son had to die! And this poor child is now without a father!'

The gentleman then translated this conversation for the benefit of everyone else in the taxi. A flood of sympathy issued. Anita felt like crying. She was amused by their quaint English, and peculiar way of expressing themselves, but she could also feel the genuineness of their feeling through it, which surprised her by its strength. So they all knew the 'Doctor-sahib'! Then how come they did not know of Sajan's death? And what was wrong with the Doctor's health? She asked them, but no one knew enough English to explain that to her. The gentleman next to her said, 'I shall show you his house. It is quite close to our kothi. His hospital is closed now, but people still go to him anyway. How unfortunate the Doctor is! Such a saintly fellow! Well, what can one do against God's will?'

Everyone said something similar and equally philosophical. God had not made a bed of roses for Anita either, but she wondered why there were so many exclamations of sorrow at the very mention of the Doctor's name.

Roorkee seemed no different from the other towns that they had passed by on the road, she thought, when she got out of the taxi. There were perhaps a few more trees, a few more open fields around it. There was a large canal just before entering the town. It must have been a famous one, since the driver had again pointed it out to her. The gentleman with her got her suitcases down and assisted her into a cycle-rickshaw. He haggled with the owner and then came and sat in it himself. When the poor, skinny rickshaw-walla, sweating under the blazing sun, started pedalling the rickshaw that pulled them and their luggage,

Anita felt such shame that she wanted to jump out of it. After about fifteen minutes, they were on the outskirts of the town. More trees, a broad road and fast trucks on the road. The gentleman next to her pointed to a compound with tall, solid walls, and said, 'Jail. Very big. Very bad people here.' He seemed proud even of the jail in his town. As she was turning her gaze away from the jail, the rickshaw came to a halt. Five or six houses stood in a row, sharing a long outer wall. In front of that wall pierced with doors, in a little space between it and the road, under scrawny trees, stood a buffalo with her calf, some donkeys, some dogs, a couple of goats, and about a dozen naked children. On seeing the rickshaw stop there, the children made an uproar, and when they noticed a strange, white woman in a dress, they yelled for their mothers to come out. Some women peeped out with their dupattas pulled over their foreheads. The gentleman approached them and said, 'Doctor-sahib's daughter-in-law!' One woman came forward and beckoned to Anita to follow her.

A slightly older boy pulled her suitcases out. Anita got down and was about to thank the gentleman but he had already climbed back into the rickshaw, which was on its way. When she saw him look back and wave and shout to her, 'See you, see you!', she too waved and followed the woman in through a door. Blinded by the sun, she could not see anything inside. But her nose took in the stench and she felt sick. She leaned against the wall waiting for her eyes to get used to the darkness inside. The woman went ahead a few paces towards the inner courtyard and waited for her. Peter hugged her neck and started crying again, perhaps frightened by the darkness and the stench. Someone from inside the room on the left asked something in a low, rough voice. The woman went in and answered hurriedly, and the same voice said something more. The woman returned to Anita and led her in, holding her hand, and then going to the other end, moved a curtain away from a hole-like window in the wall. A string-cot was visible in the light from that window, and on it a sack full of old clothes.

Or at least that's what Anita thought. When she moved closer, she saw that it was a man sleeping. Shaken by disgust, pity, amazement, and perhaps even fright, she realized that this was Sajan's father, her father-in-law, Bishambhar Singh. It was to meet this man that she had come thousands of miles as if pulled by a rope. She felt her legs give under her and she sank down on that soiled, dusty floor.

She said the first thing that came to her lips: 'Doctor Bishambhar Singh, I presume!'

Strange noises emanated from the sack on the cot and it started to shake. She realized that the man was actually laughing and then she too started to laugh. Very slowly, obviously making an effort to speak as clearly as possible, he said, 'Anita, welcome home.'

Anita's eyes filled with tears. She held Peter forth and said very quickly, 'This is Peter. Your grandson. I have named him after my father. When Sajan...When Peter...Oh...Peter was born after Sajan died. He is not a year old yet. Has just started to walk...' She stopped, at a loss for words.

Again Bishambhar said with an effort, 'Hello, Peter!' Then after a pause, 'You will get used to my speech. I cannot talk very clearly.'

Now Anita observed her father-in-law carefully for the first time. His beard was grey, his head quite bald, and his face was pulled to one side. A stroke, she realized. Was it the shock of Sajan's death? Or was it some other accident? Some other misfortune, talked about in hushed tones by her fellow travellers in the taxi? Who could tell?

Bishambhar must have said something in Punjabi. The woman, obviously used to his speech, went away.

Again slowly he said to Anita, 'It is dirty here. She will clean the other room for you. You can sleep there. There is water in the pot outside the door. The toilet is out there. She will show you.' He had trouble speaking.

Anita stood up and said hurriedly, 'Please, you don't have to talk. Doesn't anyone else speak English? I can ask someone else if I need anything.'

'Bahadur will come in the evening. He is my compounder. He will...everything...' He stopped and closed his eyes.

Hopelessly Anita stared at his grey face, grey beard, and the greyish dusty bedsheet which covered him. Again the woman came and beckoned to her. The other room was a bit brighter. Outside the door was the washroom—just a lean-to where there was a big pot filled with water. Inside the room was a bare string-cot and a frayed mat which had just been laid out on a hurriedly-swept floor. The dirt from it was piled up outside the door. When the woman once again beckoned, Anita put Peter down on the cot and went with her through the inner courtyard towards the entrance of the house. A strong stench that spread as the wooden door facing the road was opened, announced the primitive basket-toilet. Anita felt nauseated, but smiled at the woman and nodded. She was sure she could not use that toilet to save her life. What on earth was she going to do?

She came inside again and sat down near Bishambhar Singh's cot on the floor. He seemed asleep. Or maybe even unconscious, she thought in alarm. But he heard her, opened his eyes and said something.

Anita bent over him and said, 'Pardon me,' and he repeated it. With some trouble, she could make out one word, 'tea'. She looked around. No stove, no kettle. She asked, 'Would you like some tea?'

'No. For you.'

'No, thanks.'

On hearing this exchange, the woman came in again. He told her something. She went out and in about ten minutes brought in a plate and a glass. There was something like bread and a mess of vegetables on the plate. Anita did not know what it was, nor what she could give to Peter. Milk, maybe? She asked her father-in-law about milk. He called for some milk. When they brought it, he again said to Anita, one word at a time, 'Mix it with water. He won't be able to digest it otherwise.' Anita was going to ask where she could boil some water, but she gave up. So many people are drinking this water, she thought, so will Peter. She mixed milk and water together and gave it to him. Strange taste, strange place, and the terrible heat. Peter threw the bottle away. Anita had had enough. 'Suit yourself,' she said, and laying him back on the cot she came out and picked up her plate.

She found herself almost faint with hunger, but asked her father-in-law before beginning to eat, 'And what about you?' He said, 'I cannot eat that, I will get my rice soon,' and opened his mouth with an effort to show that there was not a single tooth in it. She broke a piece of the thick roti and put it in her mouth. It was tasty enough but rather dry, so, with the next piece she took a bite of the curry. She felt as if her mouth was on fire. She gasped and choked, tears starting in her eyes. Bishambhar opened his eyes and smiled. He said, 'Eat it now with water, I will ask for curd in the evening.' She was surprised that this time she could understand him so well.

Peter must have given up his protest and taken his bottle. He was silent in the next room. She took her empty plate and glass and came to the door, looking for a place to wash them. A girl saw her and called her mother, and the mother with a dupatta covering her face, came and took the plate from her hands. The stench near the door was unbearable, so Anita stepped outside. Under the dried-up tree the mother buffalo was chewing the cud. Anita went and stood near her, gazing at the trucks passing by on the road. Of course the children gathered around her, but now Anita was no longer surprised by their nakedness. If she could, she would have shed all her clothes too. The calf was asleep near its mother and so were the dogs and goats. Not a leaf moved. The only breeze was the dusty gust created by the passing trucks.

In front of her, the road with its heavy traffic; across the road, the huge compound wall of the jail; behind her, the wall enclosing the houses, pierced by their front doors and the low doors to the privies; some noise of the goings-on inside. The children were slightly shy of her but still clustered about.

What am I doing here? Who are these people? Who is the woman who brought me lunch? Could she be Sajan's sister? No. If she were Sajan's sister, she would have sat with me, she would have cuddled Peter. Why do these strangers, these neighbours attend to Bishambhar Singh? Isn't there anyone else? If Sajan had returned without marrying me, his wife would have looked after the old man. Sajan would have been alive, working, earning, perhaps the father of a couple of naked children.

Mind engrossed in such strange musings, Anita's eyes were only vaguely aware that one of the donkeys from the motley group under the tree was dragging itself slowly away from the shade. God knew why. Gradually it left the patch of shady dust and started towards the road; inch by inch it hobbled until at last it was right on the road. Anita suddenly realized what was about to happen. Half-screaming, she jumped forward, out of the circle of children around her, just as a huge, articulated trailer-truck hit the donkey and sent it sprawling to the asphalt. The truck then ran over its legs and sped on its thundering way without caring that it had hit something. Anita did not even realize that she was screaming. By the time she rushed to the donkey a couple of more trucks had gone over it. Steeling herself, she bent down to see it. Fortunately it was quite dead. The women inside the houses, shocked by her screams, came out to see, and stood watching in amazement when they realized that all the screaming and crying was over a dead donkey. She was yelling, 'Pull the donkey away! Do something! Bury it!' The women stood gawking at her, and after a while, went away not knowing what to do or say. Anita could not bring herself to do anything either; she could not pull away the carcass herself, she was not up to it. She was so exhausted and spent by now, she simply turned back, and without stopping at the tree, went straight inside the house.

An older boy came running after her, and offered falteringly, wanting to help, 'Dead! Dead! Donkey dead!' She nodded and shut the door behind her. Without glancing at the bundle on the cot she went into the other room and lay down beside Peter, trying to sleep. She soon realized that it is impossible for more than one person to sleep on a string cot. Finally she lay down on the floor, on the mat and fell into an exhausted sleep in spite of the hardness of the floor and the humming and stinging of the insects, whatever they were. She did not really feel the tears trickling down her face.

The noise of people talking woke her up. Peter had started to cry because of the noise.

When she got up and lifted him, she realized how stiff and aching her own body was. She changed Peter's clothes after washing him and splashed her own face with a little water from the big pot before coming out. She left him on the cot with a new bottle and he seemed content. She saw that a group of people were sitting on the floor next to her father-in-law's cot. They fell silent as they saw her.

One of them came forward and said, 'I am Bahadur Singh. Doctor-sahib's compounder. These are his patients.'

'Patients?'

'Yes. They still come to him. He still has the healing touch.'

Bishambhar Singh heard this, smiled crookedly and ironically tried to lift his now-useless right hand as much as he could. She only shook her head sadly, and not saying anything, sat down in a corner. He turned his attention back to his 'patients', resuming his interrupted questions. The people seemed to understand him quite well. Sometimes Bahadur would interpret. At first the people were a little shy because of her, but soon they began to speak up. One group left and another came in. Sometimes someone would give a few coins or a dirty bill, which he would accept, but if nothing was offered, he would not ask.

People kept coming in a steady stream until dusk. After talking to them Bishambhar would sometimes discuss the treatment with Bahadur in English. Anita could follow most of it, especially the medical terms. Once she even suggested something. It surprised Bahadur and he kept silent. Bishambhar said, 'You are right. But that sort of treatment is not available here. The poor folk can't go to Delhi or Bombay. Are you a doctor?'

'No. I am a microbiologist. But I work in a hospital, so I know some of these things.'

'And Sajan? What did Sajan do? Did he also work in the hospital?'

Without thinking she asked, 'Didn't you know?'

He only smiled with his crooked face. So she looked down and said, 'He used to teach at the university.'

Then she sat silent, not offering any suggestions, until all the people had left. Bishambhar was tired but when she too got up to go, he said, 'Please sit down.' With his left hand he took out a small bundle of dirty rupee-notes and coins and handing it over to Bahadur, said, 'Half is yours, give the rest to Harjit's daughter-in-law as usual, for my expenses. Give her these ten more. For two days' milk for my grandson and dinner for my daughter-in-law. Tell her to send curd and plain boiled lentils or vegetables. Our food will be too hot for Anita.'

After Bahadur left, Bishambhar turned to Anita and asked abruptly, 'Why have you come here?'

For a moment she thought of telling him that she too had been trying to find the answer since she landed. Instead she said, 'I cannot explain it.'

'I understand that, but there still must be some tangible reason that you can think of to tell me.'

She got up without a word and turned on the light. Brought out her purse from the other room and, taking out the zero-decorated check, put it into the half-open hand of her father-in-law.

'What is this?'

'It's the compensation for Sajan's accidental death.'

'How much?'

'—— dollars.'

For a while he was silent. She wondered how she would persuade him to take it if he said 'no'. How she could convince him that this was not a bribe offered to conscience. She had not committed any crime against anyone, knowingly, or unknowingly. Whether to return to India or not, whether to stay with his father or not, whether he owed it to the father or not, whether the father needed him or not—all those were Sajan's decisions. Not hers. If this father had taken the trouble to come close to his son in his childhood and youth, he would have come back in spite of her. But how often did a sense of duty prevail over an American wife, American job, American money and American life? Relationships based only on a sense of duty are no relationships at all.

As if he could hear the thoughts in her mind, Bishambhar said, 'Thank you. I can use this. It is the duty of children to look after their parents in their old age and you have fulfilled that obligation for Sajan by bringing this to me now. That is just as it should be.' He stopped to catch his breath.

Anita felt like asking, 'Why talk of duty? Did you take any trouble to be the sort of father a son would want to take care of?' But she kept quiet.

Bishambhar again answered that unspoken question: 'You do not recognize such an obligation, such a debt. You put all the old folk together in a 'home' and pay strangers to care for them. Nothing wrong in that either; for, if a man's worth is measured only in terms of his utility, there is no other option but to relegate him to limbo. Unfortunately, even here, there is only one solution at present to that problem: to be a burden to your own children. It is my great good fortune that there is no one left any more to carry my burden. I too, am cared for by strangers, in charity and for money. Now I shall divide this money into five parts. One will go to Bahadur and one to Harjit as payment for looking after me; one will pay for my food and drink, and medicines, and maybe hospitalisation and funeral; one would cover my poor patients' medical expenses; and one you should take back for Peter. Sajan did not pay his debt as a son. He refused to do that; so it is right that you, as his wife, are now doing that for him. But he also died without fulfilling his duty as a father. So now I will compensate for that a little.'

'Peter does not need anything. What I earn is enough for him,' Anita flared up.

'If you don't need it, then give it to the orphans in America. Surely there are still orphans in America?'

Anita was shocked by the cutting roughness of his reply. She had expected praise from the old man for her own thoughtfulness. Perhaps even gratitude. Both were absent from his acceptance. He was merely apportioning what he thought was his due, in a matter-of-fact manner. She saw that he understood her unspoken thought again, and smiled a little at her before closing his eyes.

When Bahadur returned to the room, Bishambhar said to her, still with his eyes closed, 'You should go back tomorrow. Bahadur will see to that. You wouldn't last long in this misery. Thank you for coming. Take care of Peter.'

And then his head lolled back as if he was exhausted. When he made an inarticulate noise, waving his useless hand, Bahadur went to him and pried the check from it. He did manage to say, 'Bank...' clearly, but all his strength seemed to have left him.

Bahadur tidied his bed, gave him a shot and started to leave. By then Anita had checked on

Peter in the other room and had come out. She said to him, 'Wait, I want to ask you something.'

He stopped, and then followed her out of the front door. He was short, she thought, much shorter than Sajan. Even with the turban he was just about her height.

'Where are the Doctor's daughters?'

'They have passed away.'

'All?'

'Yes. One passed away during childbirth at about the time Sajan went to America. One had tuberculosis, she did not last much longer after that and the last one died last year of typhoid.'

'My God!'

He did not say anything.

'Did the Doctor disown his son for marrying me?'

'Not really. They did not write to each other a lot anyway. And when he decided to settle in America, the Doctor-sahib was disappointed. After that, what was the point in writing letters to him?'

'Why was he disappointed? Because Sajan did not come back to look after his father? But priorities shift, values change; why couldn't he understand that?'

'No, it's not that simple, and certainly not that selfish. I'd rather say it was because the son did not fulfil any of his obligations...to his family, to his people, to his country...Naturally, the Doctor-sahib was disappointed. Mrs. Singh, all his life the Doctor-sahib has recognized the priority, the value only of the call of his duty; his duty to these people; he has rated his own life cheap before that, why should he try to understand any other values?'

Anita looked down. A line of ants was going somewhere in the dust. Her gaze followed it. Someone had finally pulled the carcass of the donkey away from the road and into the bordering dust. Now it was being raided by dogs, crows, ants, flies. The vultures would come soon. No one could stand to live in its stench by tomorrow. But who knows, perhaps these people are used to stenches. Used to donkeys being crushed under trucks, used to people dying of disease, in accidents and floods and epidemics. It's all a question of how much one can get used to. She thought of Bishambhar on his cot. Even when he was so nearly dead, so incapacitated, when he could not even talk properly, his poor patients were still flocking to him, and he was still caring for them the best he could.

Sajan could not understand a father who would not put his children, his comfort, even his life ahead of paying his debt to these poor people; and his father could not understand Sajan who wanted to spend his short life in the warmth of a little love, a little luxury, paying his debt to himself in the world before leaving it. In the end there remained nothing between the two but this check...

'And Peter Robert Singh, of course!' Suddenly she felt as though she held in her hand a thread that would lead her to the very centre of the maze, if only she would persevere. She went in and ate the thick roti with some boiled lentils and lay her stiff and aching body on the mat, and before falling asleep, said to Peter Robert Singh sleeping beside her, 'Remember Peter, children must look after their old parents. That debt has to be paid. One way or another.'

Translated from the Marathi original 'Dena' by Vidyut Aklujkar and the author.

Insy Winsy Spider

WHAT are 'we' when we are 'we'? It is easy enough to answer this question negatively. For instance: 'we' are not 'they', or 'he' or 'she'; nor are 'we' that book, bedsheet, shirt, bicycle, crow, dog or cat. But this is still not an answer to the original question. Psychologists say that, in the beginning, a baby cannot differentiate between itself and its mother (or any other person in the place of a mother), and that when, slowly, it begins to perceive this difference, an idea of its own self also begins to take shape in its mind.

In my own case, perhaps this process did not follow quite so smoothly, for my mother died giving birth to me and my father quickly dumped me in his sister's lap and went on his way. The world had not progressed far enough then for fathers to consider caring for their babies (not that it has now). My poor aunt did the best she could for me while caring for her own children and family; but I think, when at the age of a few days or weeks, I realized that no one had the time to run to feed me, or to change my sodden diaper even after I had been yelling lustily for a considerable time, I began to perceive quite quickly that there was an 'I' in this world and there were 'they', who mostly ignored me. It may have been due to this early indoctrination that my picture of 'myself' was strong and definite, its outlines dark and bold. I knew exactly where 'I' ended and 'others' began. But maybe this was an illusion and I did not really know myself. For if I did, I would have followed, like so many other women in my situation, a course of studies that finished quickly and earned me a job.

But instead, I went for higher qualifications in philosophy. My father, who used to visit me on holidays and feast days, found this a puzzling development. He wanted my aunt to find me a husband after I got my B.A. When I said I was going to do my M.A. in philosophy, he looked at me, obviously wondering, What *is* this creature who has been masquerading as my daughter all these years?, and asked, 'But why philosophy, Vishalakshi?' (Oh, yes, I forgot to tell you my name, undoubtedly a contributing factor to my strong sense of self: Vishalakshi Sethumadhava.

Now, isn't that a name! Of course, all but my father call me Vishu.) I answered with a superior air, 'I wish to study Buddhist philosophy.' He raised his eyebrows a little and asked, 'Hinayana or Mahayana?' I was stumped for an answer, but thought, Even a busy physician apparently seems to find time to read about these arcane matters when not saddled with a wife and children! And, not expecting an answer, he went on, 'I think you have already burdened your aunt enough. You can go on with your studies only if you get hostel accommodation, otherwise, it's marriage for you, young woman!' Not allowing my aunt to utter a few feeble protests, I answered proudly, 'Right.' With a first in B.A. I was quite sure of getting a place in the university hostel.

The HOD of philosophy was an interminable bore. The entire class used to fall asleep—with their eyes closed or open—the moment he entered. But I, who soon grasped the philosophical truth that to get where you want to be, you have first to get into the good books of HODs, was an exception to this rule. Even when my mind was fast asleep, I tutored my large eyes (those very eyes which had earned me my name, presumably) to fix themselves with serious intensity upon his face. This tactic paid off and he was soon convinced that I was an earnest, hard-working, intelligent student. After this it followed inevitably that I should make myself visible to visiting professors (especially foreign), be always eagerly underfoot during departmental seminars and such, and begin to be mentioned in footnotes of thanks for research assistance in the HOD's papers. However, even when I was busily engaged in all these activities, my aunt persisted in looking for 'suitable boys' for me; but when I in turn persisted in rudely asking some poor engineer or doctor or accountant to explain the difference between Heraclitan and Platonic concepts of 'Truth', she gave up, and so did Father. If he had again brought up the question of 'Hinayana or Mahayana', I would have told him unhesitatingly, 'Hinayana'. For by then, my M.Phil. dissertation on 'Some Problems About the Concept of Self in Hinayana Philosophy' had received rather distinguished notice in the right quarters.

And it also followed inevitably that I should then begin to teach philosophy and fall in love with another teacher of philosophy whom I met at some seminar or the other. Here I wish to note that we never asked each other such philosophical questions as 'What is the Meaning of Love?' I am also tempted to assert that in our life together we hardly said a word that did not pertain to philosophy (or perhaps just an occasional loving remark); but in truth, our marriage was no different from that of any other couple. To the usual strifes about the daily dal-and-rice, mopping up, washing up, various shortages and how to meet them, we added the stresses and strains of our professional rivalries and ups and downs. I cannot say that my refusal to give in to my husband's demands that I pay a little more attention to the above-mentioned daily strifes and little less to philosophy added to our happiness. What we did add to our life together was my daughter. In order to help her on her way to greatness, we named her Maitreyi. (All but her mother call her Mittu.) Also, in order to guard her from any confusion in her mind regarding 'self' and 'others', I kept her on a tight schedule right from birth. I am sure that the demarcating lines between 'herself' (yelling with hunger), her mother (waiting for the clock to strike three before giving her the bottle), and her father (shouting in the background, 'Will you stop that brat! I have to finish this paper today!') became quite clear in her mind at a very early age.

Funny thing was, she became most attached to my father, who had 'retired' on account of a heart attack around the time of her birth, and who was a frequent guest in our house thereafter. To tell you the truth, he more or less brought her up. I was sure that he was not telling her bedtime stories about the difference between the Hinayana and Mahayana philosophies, but mostly I ignored their childish chat. Also ignored remarks she made at the age of twelve—actually shocking enough—such as, 'Must make a separate garlic tadka for the palak, you know.' And then, at the age of eighteen, even before she got her B.A., she declared that she was going to marry the son of one of our colleagues. It was not possible to ignore that announcement. It cast a deathly pall over the house. Whatever else my husband and I disagreed upon, we were perfectly in accord about the great future we foresaw for our daughter.

He pushed away his dinner uneaten and yelled, 'What! Getting married! And who is going to do your B.A.? And M.A.?' I objected to his premise that women cannot do anything after marriage, and said, 'She will do her B.A. and M.A. after her marriage, won't you, Maitreyi?' She said, 'I am not interested in further studies.' Now I pushed away my plate as well. In one corner of my mind I whined about the timing of familial strifes which always seem to take place at the dinner table. Even if my dinners were no better than edible, I still wanted people to eat them after I had gone to the trouble of cooking them. But aloud, I said, 'Oh, great! What are you interested in, if not in studying? Become man-mad, have you? They say it's natural at this age, so let's leave that. But tell me, do you mean to do anything else in life at all?' Her father didn't give her time to answer and growled again, 'What the hell do you mean, not interested in studies? You tell me! The poor, lame, blind and stupid are struggling, panting for an education. And here are you who's got it on a platter, not interested! I don't believe this!' Now my father entered this 'discussion' and said, 'Well, if those not interested in education are out of it, those who want it will have more space, won't they?'

Oh, now I got it. A grandfather-granddaughter conspiracy. I turned to him, breathing fire, and he too pushed away his plate and said, 'Why do you always make potatoes or doodhi?' From the corner of my eye, I saw the slight nod my husband gave. It blew my temper to smithereens. I said through gritted teeth, 'I don't have time to pick over finicky, dainty vegetables. Why don't you take over the cooking? You haven't got anything else to do anyway.' My husband was taken aback by this rudeness and half-said, 'Vishu!' but Maitreyi forestalled him and said, 'I don't want to do 'anything else', Aai. I just want to get married and look after my home and family.'

That night I wept with anger and sorrow and what do you think my husband said to console me? 'It was wrong to stop after only one child. If we'd had another, we could have tried to bring it to our point of view and you wouldn't have felt so bad!' I pushed him away and turned to the wall, but kept on asking myself, 'Where did I go wrong?'

The next day I wiped my mind clean and sat down determinedly to write the paper I was to read in Bangalore: 'If the 'self' is posited as 'non-continuous' and does not journey from birth to birth, then the question arises: what is the entity that keeps awake its awareness of 'liberation' and directs its steps towards nirvana through many births?' And then suddenly I threw down the pen and stared at Maitreyi, chopping onions. It was a revelation.

The psychologists were all wrong. It is true that when a baby slowly begins to grasp the difference between itself and its mother, its awareness of its 'self' also slowly becomes stronger. But when does a mother begin to differentiate between herself and her baby? It was necessary to begin all over again. Ask: what are 'we' when we are 'we'? It is easy enough to answer this question negatively: 'I' am not this Maitreyi.

Translated from the Marathi original 'Bhijata Bhijata Koli' by the author.

Vervain

OF all the names bestowed upon Christian women, Elizabeth must surely be the one with the largest number of diminutives. From the first half you have Eliza, Liza, Lizzy, Ellie, Ella and their variations; from the second half you have Beth, Betty, Betsy, Bets and so on. There are also the more exotic ones combining the middles, the ends, the beginnings: Libby, the Good Queen's Lilibet, Elspeth, Elisheba, Bettina, Lista, Lizaveta, even such bizarre ones as Bitty and Zabby... And of course there are those Elizabeths who are called by their whole names. Indeed an infinitely variable name. But the strange thing about this name is, whatever diminutive an Elizabeth gets saddled with, it sticks to her all her life like her skin. A Betty may go to the ends of the earth to try to become a Bess, but people somehow realize that she is a Betty in spite of all her efforts to get them to call her Bess. Somehow, though all are Elizabeths, Bettys are Bettys and Besses are Besses and never the twain shall interchange or be confused or disguised.

It was her fate to be named Elizabeth, for it was also her right as the first granddaughter of her grandmother Elizabeth, who had lived all her life as a Lisbet. Lisbet, to all the family meant a certain age, a certain outline, certain foods, certain smells, certain tactile feels... There was, and could be, only the one Lisbet. So *she* could not be a Lisbet, that was for sure. And yet she had to be some sort of an Elizabeth. That name demanded resolution of the problem of what each Elizabeth was going to be. After all, it wasn't a name like 'Jane', which could hardly be anything else. And when she was born, Father, celebrating the birth of a daughter a long time after three sons, presiding over the christening feast, must have given some thought to this problem of the Elizabeths of this world. His mother, after whom the baby was named, suggested Bettina, after Goethe's near-mythical mistress, but somehow, her father knew, after one glance at the fuzzy, little bald head and the vague, colourless eyes and the fists open wide instead of closed as his sons' had been, that this was not a Bettina, nor Bess, nor Liz... This was someone special who needed a new variation on the theme, which only he could compose.

And so he raised his glass of champagne, and looked down the loaded and well-populated table at all his and his wife's family and friends, and said, 'Well, here's a toast to my little Li! May she live long and happily; and prosper.'

There was quite a confusion at the table, especially as many glasses of champagne had already been raised. Uncle Arnold thought Father had said 'Lily', Uncle Fritz thought he had said 'Marlee' and wondered what kind of name was that, Aunt Lotte—Mother's oldest sister—thought he had said 'Lotte' and was rejoicing that in this child's double name Elizabeth-Carlotta, her own and her mother's, the baby's maternal grandmother's name, Carlotta should achieve prominence. Then Mother spoke up and said, as usual, in the voice of common sense, 'Hans-Joachim, do speak up! What did you say?' And Father, a little irritated, a little put-out, said loudly and clearly, 'I said *Li*, here's to my little daughter *Li*.' Aunt Erika, Mother's younger sister, thought it sounded very Chinese and said, 'Oh, how pretty! Then together with Ta for Carlotta, she can be Li-Ta! Really exotic.' And everyone drank to the health of Hans-Joachim and Ria's little baby girl with the strange name of Li-Ta. No one who called her by her name ever forgot that hyphen, and so, it did sound very much like a two-syllable Chinese name.

In time, she became quite proud of it for she knew that her name was unique, that there was no other Elizabeth in the world with precisely that diminutive, which was bestowed upon her by her adored father.

But as luck would have it, her childhood, like that of all children born in 1935 in Germany, slid slowly and irrevocably into hardship, deprivation, flight, and fight for survival; and in later life she could conjure up no pretty memories to go with the pretty, unusual name. It was not easy growing up in Germany in the turbulent late thirties. Father and her eldest brother (Hans-)Ernst went off to 'war', and one by one most of her uncles and cousins too. And many died; even Ernst, she supposed, because Mother got a telegram one day and then was never the same again. Much later she was to wonder if this was because he was a son, or because he was the first-born. (First-borns were special, as she discovered eventually for herself.) Father, thank God, was all right. But they worried. If the war went on and on the other two, Franz(-Joachim) and Arnold(-Christophe), named after the uncles and the grandfathers who were now dead, would grow old enough to be drafted.

And the war did go on, and then they had to move and hide in a new place where no one knew the real ages of the boys, who, due to wartime deprivations had remained a bit stunted anyhow. They left the house they were all born in, and most of what was in it. They thought Li-Ta was just a baby, and it was Mother and the boys who really missed the house, the streets, the city and all they were used to. However, unknown to anyone, she too must have missed the smells and the feel and the sounds of the house. For she became fretful and troublesome and sickly, and no one guessed she was pining. (Everyone supposed she was too little, yet she remembered all this years later when she was in therapy.) And they were safer in the 'country' from bombs and things than in the city. They went to live on a farm. They worked as farmhands and domestic help. The farmer and his sons had died in the war and his wife had no one to help her. Then commenced a war of their own: for food. That farm hardly grew anything and the woman had given up on it long ago. She just took them in because 'they' said she had to. She didn't care about the land, she didn't care about them, she didn't care about anything. She just sat in her kitchen, rocking in an old rocking chair and ate whatever Mother cooked for her—whatever they could scrape together, growing, begging, scrounging. There was the endless digging and planting and digging again for potatoes, turnips, swedes. There were the miles and miles of trekking, trapping, gathering berries and leaves and mushrooms and other stuff that grew in bushes and scrub round about; there were even queues in the village, for sugar, for lamp-oil; there was the unending hard work, not just for Mother and Franz and Arnold, but even for her (she was nearly eight after all, and was expected to chip in—begging for a few more handfuls of grain, a couple more potatoes...).

There was never enough to eat. She forgot what meat tasted like. They all looked like scarecrows. At least she supposed they did, because Mother and Franz and Arnold did, and though it had been years since she had looked into a mirror, she was sure she looked just like them. And then apparently the war was over, because one day a scarecrow looking even worse than them stood on their doorstep and said he was Father. Mother held it in a half-embrace, not even able to cry any more and the children just shrank away. After a few futile efforts, Father gave up trying to entice them any closer. They even managed to return to 'their' house eventually, but by that time it was unrecognizable, either because there was nothing in it and everything smashable had been smashed and everything cartable had been carted away; or because all of them had really forgotten what it had looked like.

Even in therapy, much, much later, she was unable to remember those early years in that empty home, so successfully had she blotted them out. She only remembered that Mother died; and at the age of ten, she became mother, companion, chatelaine, cook-housekeeper, confidante and advisor to three men; the youngest of whom was twelve years older than her and the oldest close to sixty. They had nothing and no one but her in their ruined lives in a ruined home in a ruined city in a ruined country (and as far as she knew, in a ruined world). She was their Li-Ta, their everything. And they were her everything too. She didn't even bother to go to school with any regularity. It was not until Franz and Arnold left for—respectively—Canada and Australia, and after Father died, when she was twenty, that she resumed academic studies interrupted at the age of five by The War. She doggedly went through the whole lot, gymnasium and baccalaureate, and then went to the Sorbonne (because she thought Paris might be interesting) for her Master's in history, at the age of thirty-five. In her class were her twenty-something colleagues, the post-war generation, mostly girls, with whom she never felt close or comfortable. Besides, being a German in post-war France brought trials and tribulations she had not dreamed of. She was often tempted to say, 'But I was just a child of five or six or nine,' but gritted her teeth and kept silent. She remembered how Father—no more than an accountant in the Wehrmacht—was always stonily silent about his experiences as a prisoner of war. She felt as if she were a prisoner of war too, now, so long after The War.

All this no doubt had something to do with her marriage to her own Hans-Joachim, a half-Serb, half-Ukrainian, twelve years older than her; a sailor half-brother of a roommate studying history with her at the Sorbonne. (She always thought that all these halves were a great factor in his life.) And so she was gratefully relieved when, after their marriage, he joined a shipping company in Luxembourg and shifted to that haven of neutrality with her. Though not willing to go as far as her brothers to put The War behind her, she was glad not to live in countries where The War had done so much damage and mattered so much and feelings ran so high. Her brothers came over for the wedding and thoroughly approved of her choice. She was grateful to the whole lot of them. To this Hans-Joachim, not only for restoring her to herself, but for restoring her remaining family of 'men' to her; and to them for taking her back, for allowing her to be 'their' Li-Ta again, at least in a small measure, for taking this new Hans-Joachim to their hearts. After that there were bi-annual visits from Canada and Australia and weekly phone-calls. She was in touch with all she ever wanted to be in touch with.

Her wandering came to a stop at last. Her brothers generously gave up their right to that old house and she sold it. Not looking back, not grieving. Determinedly making a new beginning. With that money and some loans, they bought a house in their new country; a house with an attic and a bit of land around it, planted with good fruit trees, and even a ridiculous handkerchief of a lawn in the front. They were going to have to pay for it for years to come, but oh, the heavenly delight of it! She managed to begin to forget 'the home' she never actually remembered.

And finally, there came along 'her' boys. Her very own. In their names she got rid of all the Hanses and Ernsts and Christophes and Arnolds and Joachims who had been so great a part of her childhood and who had betrayed her by dying in The War or after; or, if not, had eventually abandoned her, their Li-Ta, for a life far away; Li-Ta to whom they had raised glasses of champagne so long ago. That was all gone and forgotten. Even this Hans-Joachim who had given her all this could not change her mind. She decided that 'her' boys—and they were all hers!—would be Paul and Mark.

And she cautiously discovered that she could allow herself to feel that she was happy, perhaps for the first time since she was five. True, she was not Li-Ta any more; but she was Maman, to all three of them, and that was just as satisfactory; once again, she was everything to three men; once again, it was enough. And the world was not in ruins at all.

And days and months and years went by and there was nothing but happiness and contentment. Apples and blackberries ripening in the back garden in a mild spring, summer roses, a maple she had nursed shedding red, red leaves in autumn, snow lying across the lawn as friends came over for a Christmas dinner, the wonderful and 'touristy' fondues and rostis she organized with the boys in the cozy winters—as wonderful as the picnics she got up under the apple trees in the spring.

Hans-Joachim did begin to travel a lot as he rose in the hierarchy, but that was good too, and she was busy at home bringing up the boys. Far too soon, they were nearly men and had wonderfully frivolous and fluffy girlfriends about whom they had good laughs with their Maman. And she would pretend to get the girls mixed up—the Paulas and the Rosas and the Dorotheas and the Sandras—and the boys would say, laughing, 'No wonder Maman, they are all rather alike anyway!' and she would be gratified and relieved that they might wander over the weekend but always returned to Maman on Monday. She was reasonable and did not wish to tie them to her apron strings. Boys will be boys, after all.

But it was a nasty shock to her to discover that her major boy too, was busy being a boy in various parts of the world while she stayed home and had a great time as usual with the other two. Oh, yes, it was a major disaster. It was so long since she had met disasters, she did not know how to deal with them. For the first time in many years, the phone wires to Australia and Canada sizzled with real words and real emotion.

And it was a shock too, to discover that Franz-Joachim and Arnold-Christophe really thought she was being silly. Boys will be boys, they said, implying that they had been boys in their time, and would be, if opportunity offered. 'He's ok,' they said, 'he loves you, he provides for you and the boys, he has given you a fine home and he is a fine man; all that is just a pastime, a divertimento, darling, so what's all this nonsense?' Though she asked them to, her brothers would not let their wives speak to her until she was calmer, over and done with this hysterical tantrum.

In despair, she took the bold step of turning to her sons. *They* were really 'her' boys after all. Paul, the elder, only said, 'Oh, come on, Maman!' and refused to discuss the matter further; and Mark, more serious, said, 'You'd better get him tested for AIDS and the like before you sleep with him again Maman!'

She wept at the humiliation of it. In sheer spite, and also self-defence, she did get him tested, but the joy was gone. The apples and blackberries did not bloom for her, nor the friends gather around in happiness. Every male friend had to be scrutinized and the question reverberated in her mind, 'Perhaps you too?' And her eyes met the wives' eyes and the condescending camaraderie she had always felt for them out of her unalloyed happiness gave way to fury as they showed pictures of their grandchildren.

And in the midst of this turmoil, Hans-Joachim announced one day that he was inviting an Indian colleague and his wife home for dinner. Li-Ta felt panic-stricken. She had no concept of India at all. She did not know what to cook, what to wear, what to say. Hans-Joachim just laughed at her and said they were only people after all. So she hurriedly ransacked the local library for information and read that most Indians were vegetarians. She hardly knew any vegetarian dishes. She bought a book and did the best she could. She expected her guest to be a woman like the ones in all those pictures she had seen in magazines and on TV and was astonished to find herself face to face with a large, gruff, assertive, jeans-clad woman about her own age. And dinner was a success.

'You are Li-Ta and I am DT,' the woman said, when they got cozy over the washing up. 'Now tell me about yourself.' And Li-Ta said, 'Well, I will. Why not start with my name?' And the strange woman listened and laughed and made tart remarks and asked finally, 'But why aren't you doing anything about history? There's so much to do! We have to write a whole new history. I mean who the hell cares about all these Charlemagnes, and Barbarossas, and Williams and Napoleans and, for that matter, from my neck of the woods, Chandraguptas and Ashokas and

Akbars and Shivajis and all the 'boys'? Let's find out what the world is really about, Li-Ta, and you can come along and burrow in the archives for us! Come on!'

And for the first time in her life, she felt that there was an 'us', whether she liked it or not. Maybe being Father's and brothers' little Li-Ta was not enough, being her boys' Maman was not enough. She had to get together with all of the 'us' who had suffered war, famine, oppression, betrayal; and suffered because boys will be boys, after all. 'They' wanted to 'make important' and play with their toys while 'we' were nothing but the little Li-Ta left at home; the little one with the special name that they could remember while they blew each other up—the Lili Marlenes, Betty Grables, Lauras and Sarahs (Li-Tas and Seetas, the strange woman DT said. Or was it Dee-Tee?— there was some secret meaning to that name because she had laughed as she told it). 'Come on, Li-Ta, there's work to do,' she said, drying the last spoon and keeping it in its place.

And Li-Ta looked at her and held her breath for a moment and then sighed and said, 'Why don't you go out and sit under the apple tree? It's lovely this time of the year. I have taken so much trouble over it, but it's worth it. Or you could wander through my blackberry patch and pick a few to eat. It's a wonderful garden. I spend so much time in it working, my back's practically broken! But I love it. I'm sure you will too. You go along. I'll just set the table for tomorrow's breakfast and lay out the boys' pyjamas on their beds and start the coffee in case they want any. I guess I had better set out the brandy glasses too. But then I'll make some vervain tea for us and bring it out to you. We'll sit out and sip it quietly. I make it at home myself, you know. It's soothing to the nerves. I don't know if it's just an old wives' tale, but it sure makes me sleep. I take a cup every night. Better than the pills my therapist prescribed. Did I tell you I am in therapy? A wonderful boy. He loves my vervain tea too. I take a few sachets for him every week. And over the tea we'll chat some more. I've loved chatting to you, telling you about myself. You know, I never had a girlfriend. I find girls uncongenial. I much prefer the boys. Don't you?'

The woman looked at her and her face became blank for a moment and she almost corrected her, saying neither of them was a 'girl' any more, but then paused and said instead, 'No. I don't. But do let's sit out under the apple tree and drink vervain tea. Why not? We all need to sleep after all, and some of us more than others, so why not?'

And after Li-Ta finished all the chores for the comfort of her boys, her nightly routine fifty years of her life, whether the boys were Hanses and Joachims and Franzes and Arnolds or Pauls and Marks, she made vervain tea and took it out and she and her guest sipped it in silence, listening to the apple-blossoms fall.

But, for all the vervain, it was almost daybreak before Li-Ta fell asleep that night. So she got her therapist, another of her Wonderful Boys, to prescribe a really strong pill for her the next time she saw him.

Rose Jam

WELL, of course there is such a thing as rose jam. It was not at all rare, while I was growing up, to find a large jar of it tucked away in most pantries. It was doled out by all grandmothers on very hot summer days to ward off the ill effects of heat. The reason I thought I would begin this account with it is, it's the only really exotic thing about my childhood I can put my finger on: I was brought up eating a jam of roses. You see, over the last few years I have come across a lot of books written by talented writers who left their countries of origin around puberty to settle down in America or Canada or Australia or wherever, and who, before leaving the mother countries, seem to have had enchantingly strange childhoods quite unlike mine, humdrum in retrospect and in comparison. In these books the authors, their parents, grandparents, siblings, schoolmates and surroundings appear so exotic and magical as to be unrecognizable, in spite of the fact that I am quite sure I have ridden the bus and trodden the streets in a few of the spots described; and very probably, though unknowingly, in the company of those same exotic characters.

As a result of the publication and popularity of these tomes more and more people I meet expect me to have ridden a camel, an elephant, a horse, at least a bullock cart to school (I rode the bus, of course); or to have been forced into marriage by my cruel parents at a young age to a man whose face I saw for the first time when the priests drew apart the silken veil between us at the auspicious moment on my wedding day (we had been living together for two years without occasioning any serious comment or opposition before agreeing to marry); to have had strange rituals performed on me upon first 'becoming a woman'(all I got was a newspaper-wrapped package of sanitary napkins thrust at me by a mother busy planning her next field-trip to study some tribe or the other in northeast India); or at the very least, to possess scores of brothers and sisters with exotic names such as Jasmine-flower, Eternal happiness, Lotus-eyes or Beautiful morning (in India too, names are just names and hardly ever given with a view to their meanings as it is difficult to predict if a couple-of-weeks-old infant is likely to grow to live up to the meaning of any given name, however meaningful). And so I am made to feel quite uninteresting and unacceptable as an authentic Indian in foreign parts. Disappointed friends and acquaintances accuse me of not being Indian enough though I have been Indian since the moment of my birth and have never left the country of my origin to settle anywhere else. True, I have spent a lot of my adult life wandering around the world in the wake of a wandering husband but during all such wanderings I have always felt decidedly Indian in spite of appearances to the contrary (I am generally to be found in jeans and tees rather than in gracefully flowing saris, and my hair is chopped off to the point of non-existence). So I thought I had better put in a word for the millions of Indians like myself who are not in the least exotic and yet are perfectly Indian (just let them try and get a visa from any of the above-mentioned immigrant-havens), who had run-of-the-mill childhoods and who never got around to writing bestselling books about the special ingredients that went into Grandmother Goddess-of-Wealth's special curry.

So, because I wanted to capture your interest right away, dear reader, I hit upon the rose jam. And also because this is a story about my grandmothers, one of whom introduced me to this delicacy, and both of whom must carry, rose jam and all, the responsibility for their descendants not being interestingly 'oriental'.

First off, neither of my grandmothers was particularly interested in cooking, let alone in special and spicy curries with secret ingredients in them. My mother's mother, Aai, the rose jam-maker, had at least the rudiments of everyday cooking and pickle-jam-and-sweet-making; my father's mother, Baya, was a dead loss. Her cooking consisted of throwing everything she intended to have for dinner into one pot and adding whatever spices struck her fancy that day. According to my father, most of the time he and his brothers ate the damned stuff only because they were so hungry. In fact it was this pathetic mess revealed to Aai in my father's lunch box (when he accompanied my mother's brother, a college friend, to his home one day) that moved her to invite him to eat at her place whenever he wanted. This generous gesture led to the romance between my father and my mother and eventually to their marriage in the teeth of opposition by her parents. His parents were not opposed to it for the simple reason that they could not summon up enough interest in so trivial a matter as their son's marriage. They were social workers and had many other important things to do, such as change India's unjust social structure, eradicate the caste system, care for orphans and educate widows.

You can see how this is a perfectly commonplace occupation for one's grandparents. I would be far more courted at cocktail parties if they were considerate enough to have been maharajas, even minor princelings, if not prime ministers to royalty, or royal confidants, at least brave warriors in India's struggle for freedom, bigoted brahmins or downtrodden untouchables. But they were simply social workers. An unusual enough occupation in that place at that time, but hardly the stuff on which one could dine out. And don't let Aai's penchant for making rose jam fool you into thinking that there at least you would meet with a truly representative, traditional, last-century Indian lady. No sir. That intrepid soul followed her husband to Burma when he took up a job there on behalf of the government. Barely into her teens, totally illiterate, she, who had never been outside her village let alone country, took up abode among strangers in a strange and far off place and there gave birth to and brought up her five sons and my mother. Now, I certainly feel that these grandmothers of mine led interesting and exciting and adventurous lives. But they were not, alas, interesting in an exotic way. And what is more damning is that they were interesting in a western, non-Indian way, thus relegating me, their descendant, equally given to the untraditional pastimes of globetrotting, and taboo-breaking, to a uniform greyness in the eyes of her acquaintances all over the world.

However, to resume Aai's story: according to her, a few of her children died on the way, but by the time I came along to ask her about it, she had forgotten how many. She said they were all sons though, and so my mother, the only daughter, was the 'pupil in the eye' of her parents and her brothers. This is significant in later developments. Because my mother, rich and beautiful and a rare prize to be won on the marriage market, could have looked as early and as high as she chose, for a husband. But all she ever wanted out of life was knowledge and education, more and more of it, much more than fathers in those far off days were willing to give to their daughters, however indulged.

Aai's support could not be counted on either, though by this time she had managed to learn to read and write, along with her children and with their help. She could read not only our own language, but also quite a bit of English. Once when I asked her who taught her to read English, she said, 'Your grandfather of course. You see, there wasn't much to do in that hole of a place in Burma, so he used to while away evenings teaching me to read and write and do sums.' It seems he used to read Somerset Maugham aloud to her. As an aside, this habit of reading aloud in the evenings carried on in our family. I remember all of us reading aloud to my parents from Jane Austen; and in the holidays, which I spent with my cousins, reading aloud to my great-uncle in the mornings while he stropped his straight razor and shaved himself. Being a Cambridge man he would correct my pronunciation with severe contempt, but to no avail as I have retained my distinctly Indian accent to this day. Naturally my grandmother thought that if she could manage to read and write without going to school, her daughter had no reason to go outside the home and pursue such unnatural goals as higher education.

My mother was determined, however, and to further her educative process she hit upon a novel idea around the age of twelve, taking advantage of her father's and her brothers' severe handicap in being mere males. Though her father was willing to let her go to school 'until she became a woman', he was bent upon restricting her to the house after that to learn homemaking skills from her mother until he found a suitable husband for her. My mother was not about to get married at twelve. After the exam results came in and she found that she had passed yet another grade with flying colours, she proceeded to lock herself in the family bath (which, according to the ideas of hygiene then prevailing, was way removed from the house and contained heaps of firewood to heat the bath water) and refused to come out until her father agreed in the presence of all her doting brothers to let her continue one more year. With six quite helpless males worrying themselves sick over her starving to death after being without food for three whole hours, and over the presence of rats in the woodpile, and over the effect of the dark upon her sensitive mind and of the damp upon her delicate health, the battle was won even before it was joined. She continued in this manner year after year until she graduated from high school, and by then her father had so far reconciled himself to the inevitable as to agree without demur to let her go on to college.

This, though not at all unusual in the rest of the world, was quite a rare and wonderful privilege in those days for a woman in India. I am afraid I cannot boast of an illiterate but instinctively wise mother either, whose calm and traditional counsel always stood me in good stead. She was not a calm sort of person and her traditional wisdom took the form of knowing better than to offer counsel to daughters as headstrong and wilful as herself. I know I would be a more acceptable Indian to my foreign friends (and even to my Indian ones, I sometimes feel) if at least she had gone to school on an elephant, but she rode to school on a bike until her graduation, when she met and married my father and then went on to Berlin University for her postgraduate studies, so I assume that she went to classes there on a streetcar.

Anyway, as I said, my father was a severe disappointment to my mother's parents. There wasn't anything wrong with him, you understand. He just wasn't good enough for their precious daughter. He was a lecturer at her college and a friend and tennis partner of her elder brother's. And so romance blossomed and she must have resorted to the old bathroom trick, because her father agreed without too much fuss to let her marry the man of her choice. His consent was given in spite of the fact that he had any number of objections to my father. First of all, to him, my father's parents were not quite respectable. I mean, social workers? And besides, my father's father had courted and married Baya after her first husband had died. (Sorry, no forcing-into-marriage-by-cruel-father, etc. here either.) This marriage was perfectly legitimate as far as the law of the land was concerned (British law) but not at all acceptable to religion and society; so, for all practical purposes, my father and his brothers were bastards no matter what the law said. And a lecturer? You've got to be joking. Did she know how much money he made? How would she, a rich man's only daughter, manage on peanuts? But my mother was not interested in all this stuff. She wanted to marry my father and that was that. Unexpectedly, she found an ally in her mother. Though Aai had not been at the forefront of those who gave in to her daughter's previous hunger-strikes, this time she took her side because she liked my father. I remember her as a stern and cantankerous woman, not easy to please or get along with. But I also remember that she had always been very fond of my father, and quite often relieved him of the task of looking after us whenever Mother was off to various corners of the world in her everlasting quest for more knowledge.

It was during Aai's sojourns with us in my mother's absence while I was still a child that I learnt whatever I do know about mildly exotic, traditionally Indian medicines like rose jam for heatstrokes, calendula juice for earache, lemongrass tea for colds, aloe pulp for coughs and other such home remedies, electuaries, lotions and potions. She tried to smear turmeric paste on our faces to improve our complexions, but I was not having any of that. She found me a great trial. I insisted on wearing shorts like the neighbourhood boys I ran around with, climbed trees and hills, pelted people and animals with pebbles from my slingshot, beat up any poor soul who crossed me, used rude words, had lice in my hair, plasters on my knees and braces on my teeth. There was no way she could have taught me those homemaking skills, the learning of which her own daughter had shrugged off. She soon gave up.

Perhaps if I had paid her more heed then, I would now know how to make all those delectable

Indian sweets and spicy hot curries. I would be able to glide along gracefully in silk. I would have long dark tresses that I would know how to perfume with sandalwood smoke. I would have a dusky golden complexion which I would keep clear with esoteric Indian pastes made of herbs and flowers. If only I could have seen into the future, where such attributes and talents would have stood me in good stead! But, in my blindness, I told her that she had done pretty well what she pleased including socially unacceptable things like learning to read and write English and she had encouraged her daughter to do what she pleased, marry whomever she wanted and go abroad for studies; she had no right to make me into a demure little homebody. She was left without an argument and when she took the matter up with my mother, of course my mother impatiently said, 'Well, I don't know how to cook or sew and it hasn't mattered a whit, has it?' And that ended all attempts at making a proper young lady out of me.

At times Aai could be heard to mutter (after being particularly annoyed with me) that I must take after my father's family. But this indictment was only half-hearted, and never uttered in the hearing of Baya, because only the most foolhardy person would have cared to lock horns with her. Now, let me tell you, Baya was a real eccentric. She died when I was ten so I don't remember much about her. On the other hand I remember my father's father very well. He lived most of his later life in our house. As he lived to be over a hundred, there was a lot of life left in him still when I came along, the last of his grandchildren. And he lived with us very peacefully. But his wife could not get along with any of her daughters-in-law. After bickering and quarrelling and rendering life impossible for her mild husband and her equally mild sons, she made it necessary for a family-council to be called to find for her problem an unusual solution. And it convinced everybody of the truth of what they had always suspected: we were an eccentric family, importers of unnecessary ideas into a country already replete with them.

The situation was resolved in the following manner: my grandfather had devoted his active life to the cause of furthering the education of women in India, during the course of which he had founded a university for women at the turn of the century. Though a lot of changes had occurred after his retirement—and a number of industrial houses, and after Independence, the government, had endowed this university—his name was indelibly associated with it and he was a much-honoured and frequent guest at all its Public Days. One of the campuses of this university lay no further than a mile from our house. It was decided by him, and announced at the family council that as a favour to its founder, this university's hostel near our house would harbour his troublesome wife. Amazingly enough, Baya thought this a marvellous idea too, and happily went off to stay in the hostel and bully a hundred young women, and lord it over the matron and make life a burden for the principal and the cooks. I remember being sent there on a duty visit to her. She found me a perfect nuisance, dug up the obligatory sweet (which had turned black through disuse) and shooing me away, plunged back thankfully into the intrigues of that community of women. Sending off an old person to stay out of the family home into an institution is not a novel idea in the west and would not have occasioned comment. But in India! Without knowing how much their actions were to damage the image of their granddaughter in years to come, my grandmothers had been moving in the wrong direction. They may have taken the small steps that led India into the modern age, but that is because surely they did not know that no one else in the world wanted India to be anything but the quaint outpost of the Raj.

I was too small to have much to do with Baya when she was alive; but when I grew up, I read the autobiography she had dictated to my aunt a few months before her death. I could see then, that just like Aai, she was a redoubtable lady, quite up to facing ostracism, abuse, physical danger, poverty, loneliness and humiliation for what she and her husband believed in. What they believed in was the right of widows to be considered human beings by a society which had hitherto thought of them as convenient domestic and even sexual slaves. They wanted widows to be able to educate themselves, support themselves, live independently if they wanted, or marry again if they chose, to start another and richer life at a mature age. When they married each other, they were in a state of sin as it were, in the eyes of society, so on top of all the other indignities and dangers they had to face, they could not hire a house to live in. They solved the problem by moving outside the city a few miles to a haunted heath and setting up a few huts there for their own family and for other outcasts like themselves. From this beginning eventually emerged the women's university and an orphanage.

Baya had described how she used to walk seven miles to the city each evening after work during the last months of her pregnancies (in order to stay in a maternity hospital at night), walk back every morning if the baby was not born during the night and take up her daily chores in the house and the school. It's a wonder that my uncles and my father were not born on the street. One of the few things she says she regretted not having in life was a daughter. In order to compensate for this lack, she not only collected many stray 'daughters', but also dressed my youngest uncle in girls' clothes until he was old enough to go to school. One would think that a woman, so hungry for a daughter, would get along fine with her daughters-in-law when they came along; but no way. She just never got along with anybody if she could help it. Hence she was never much loved, but she was surely respected and trusted.

When my eldest uncle wanted to go to England to get his M.D., it was obvious that his parents could not afford it. There simply wasn't any money. His entire school and college education (and for that matter, that of his two younger brothers) had been managed on scholarships. But Baya was not daunted. She went walking back to the city to the grain merchant from whom she had been buying the meagre supplies needed for her home and school for years and asked him for the money. She said, 'When my son is a doctor, he will pay you back.' And that man advanced her the money without any surety other than her word. Of course my uncle paid him back; but she had also made another stipulation: each brother must pay for the education of the next, and it would be my youngest uncle who would pay back the grain merchant's loan. And so it was. The loan paid for my eldest uncle's M.D., he paid for my father's Ph.D. from Leipzig, my father paid for my youngest uncle's M.Ed. from Leeds and the grain-merchant waited, knowing that Baya's sons would pay back his loan.

Though Baya did not seem to have been the sort of person who established loving one-on-one relationships, she obviously had large sympathies. An orphan, a struggling young widow, a starving child would always arouse her to instant action; the action being simply to pick up and bring that poor thing home. For a woman who hardly had the wherewithal to feed her own husband and sons, this was generosity of the most profligate type. How she managed, God knows, and also her long suffering friends and acquaintances. She would pester anybody she thought malleable enough into giving a little something towards her charity. She would march up to a shopper in a crowded shop, the merest acquaintance, and say loudly, 'What do you need two new saris for? Anyway, now that you have bought these, you might as well give two old ones to me.' And she generally got them.

However, Baya thought us all quite uninteresting because we were not orphans in need of her charity and support. She was not about to waste her energies upon us. As a grandmother she was nothing to write home about. The one who could be relied upon for grandmotherly behaviour was Aai. She generally came to stay with us during our summer holidays because that was the only time Mother, who was a college teacher, was free to do her own research and took off for far corners of the country. Summer was also the time to make the annual supply of pickles and jams. Aai made vast quantities of these so as to give them to her five sons as well as us, and so enlisted the aid of all the grandchildren from all the beneficiary households.

I was not crazy about being put to work in my holidays, especially not on the rose jam. One had to get up very early, while the dew was still on the flowers. The flowers had to belong to only one variety of rose: the very thorny, indigenous, deep pink, heavily fragrant one with fleshy petals. My father, an enthusiastic gardener in his spare time, had planted a few of these rose bushes in our garden. So we would be hauled out of bed, made to wash and sent off with baskets to bring in the heavily scent-laden roses, only the fully open ones, without spilling too much of the dew. Aai would then separate the petals and lay them in a thick layer at the bottom of a stout glass jar with a wide mouth. On top of this layer she would lay rock candy, roughly pounded and mixed with a bit of colloidal coral (don't ask me what that is, or what it does; it was a sort of a grainy ash and had to go in). Then she would cover this with another layer of rose petals, and another of sugar mixture, until the jar was full. Then she would put it on the roof where it would catch the fierce summer sun and slowly cook itself and settle into a sticky jam at the bottom of the jar. The next day she would send us off for more roses and begin another layer. This would go on until the jam had no further to settle and the jar was full. Then she would cover it with wax paper and muslin, and stopper and store it in the darkest corner of the fascinating pickle cupboard in the pantry. The next summer the jar would be opened and each of us would be given a spoonful of this heavenly mixture in the morning, after breakfast, before we were sent out on our annual pickle-errands or allowed out in the sun to play. Any given summer we would be eating the mixture we had helped her put down the previous summer. I am certain it is only on account of this wonderful remedy that I never had heatstroke, sunburn, headache or nosebleed throughout those carefree, out-of-doors summers.

And then, as they say, the years passed. My grandparents died, I grew up and gave no end of trouble to my poor parents just as Aai had predicted, and the time came for them both to accept visiting professorships at Berkeley. I was just getting into my late teens, and, considering my track record there was no way they were going to leave me behind on my own. As it turned out, taking me with them to California was not the best of solutions. At first I wondered at the exhortations of the orientation counsellors to wear my 'ethnic' clothes. The 'ethnic' clothes were necessary, we were told, for dark-skinned foreign students, because there existed in California a slight prejudice against Mexicans, for whom we might be mistaken and mistreated.

Later, I was staggered at the euphemisms in that statement because I found out that no matter what I wore, people who are prone to be prejudiced were savagely prejudiced against anyone and everyone the slightest bit different from them, and moreover, expressed this prejudice freely with a righteousness worthy of the unjust and structured society in India against which my poor grandparents had struggled so hard and so vainly half a century ago. So, arguing with inimitable logic that folk were going to be nasty to me no matter what I did, I abandoned forever the graceful saris, the long tresses, the bangles-baubles-beads and maidenly demeanour Aai had tried to force on me, and took happily to jeans, tees, keds, chopped-off hair, boyfriends, rattle-traps, drive-ins, lovers' lanes, Renoir retrospectives, sit-ins in front of Dwinell, sneaked smokes, heckling Jimmy Hoffa and cheering Kennedy and whatever else you can think of at Berkeley just as it was getting ready to go into the unforgettable sixties. No one thought I was an Indian, but most did remark upon my 'funny' accent, so I explained it by saying that I was an

Indian, and got a foretaste of things to come: Oh, then why aren't you wearing one of those sari things? And why is your hair not long and plaited? And are you people allowed to go out of your country? And aren't your women supposed to cover their faces? And did you go to school on an elephant? And...? After fending the first of this lot with reasonable good humour and unbelievable patience, I gave up and said, 'Oh, is my accent funny? Well, so is yours.' And though that annoyed them, it also shut them up. Once when I said Indian, I was taken to be an American Indian, so I said, 'No, the real one that Columbus set out to find before losing his way,' and that met with a blank stare and silence too.

It was not long before my parents found out that I was not a virgin as I used to be when I set out from home and they despaired about me. In spite of all their westernized ways and belief in the personal liberty of an eighteen-year-old, they were, after all, a pair of Indian parents who had had centuries of traditional mores dinned into their psyches about how important virginity is. They tried to get me to marry the boy responsible, but I was not about to marry an American teenager whose head was full of nothing much but sex and junk cars and wheedling some money out of his father for an electric guitar. It was time to go home and my parents hauled me home with them, heaving sighs of relief, and I wasn't sorry to return. For I had discovered that I did not like being on the defensive for what I was.

I was not exotic, oriental or freakish enough without putting on what I thought of as a disguise. And if I refused to put on that disguise, I was just a foreign nobody with a peculiar accent. People were not comfortable with me because they could not put me into a neat category. I was not like other Indians, I was not like other foreigners, and I certainly was not like the Americans. They didn't like that. They didn't like it that I was more grown-up than their average kid, that I didn't mind giving as good as I got, that I, a foreigner from what they had been taught was an underdeveloped country, was not amazed and grateful at being allowed to enter and live in their wonderfully developed one. But they were stumped for an answer when asked why people from this underdeveloped country should have been asked to come to theirs to teach them something. And though they resented my being eager to go home from what they thought was paradise, I am sure they would have resented even more my wanting to stay on.

They made a point of telling me at all times how American society was free and easy and not bound by rules like my own, yet they thoroughly disliked my breaking those invisible rules which decreed how a humble foreigner should behave. They did not like my laughing at them and their preconceptions about me. They did not like the idea that I might marry one of their golden boys and yet they were hurt when they found out that I did not want to.

    I still remember my poor Californian boyfriend, blond hair and grey eyes and thin lips and tight smile, and all, in his Marine ROTC uniform. He made friends with me before he realized that I was supposed to be an exotic, and was surprised that I took milk and sugar in my coffee. He thought that was the only exotic thing about me, whereas I found him totally exotic, like California fruit. And now if I want to turn the tables on my foreign friends, I tell them that they all seem terribly exotic to me, which annoys them since they cannot return the compliment, as even my grandmothers were not exotic. But just consider: mangoes, bananas, sapotas, custard-apples and guavas are a pound a penny; peaches, pears, apples and plums are exotic! Dark, black-haired, midnight-eyed, hawk-nosed, pout-lipped men litter the streets; blond, grey-eyed, snub-nosed, baby-faced, pale boys are exotic, right? And, going back to the golden California boy, I decided once to try on him the only really exotic thing about me I know: I was brought up on rose jam. He didn't believe me, of course.

Morgan in Disguise

MY head was full of a lot of silly ideas about rural India before I actually went to live and work there. In the event they all proved to be just that: fondly romantic ideas conceived in childhood holidays and nursed through adulthood as soft and green patches against the big-city iron that had invaded all parts of my soul. For instance, I thought that people here would somehow be more 'real', that is, more open, frank, honest, simple, loyal and so on. This was rubbish. They were just people, full of infuriating contradictions or endearing inconsistencies, depending on your point of view. Compensating for drawbacks they did not share with their city-dwelling comrades, they had others, peculiarly their own. One of these was a total disregard of diurnal time. Time here could be measured in no less a unit than one week. Even this was due to the growth of a small town within walking distance and its institution of an open-air Sunday market. It was therefore possible for me to tell the workers on my farm to do something before Sunday. If I told them to do it today, they smiled, nodded and agreed but did not increase the ponderous pace of their endeavour.

And they did not, contrary to my expectation, display profound 'traditional' wisdom. The equivalent here of the on-line, smart-aleck, instant knowledge gleaned from the net, TV, magazines, and newspapers was superstition (such as: all snakes were poisonous, the clucking of geckos brought bad luck, or a flight of dragonflies rain). When I pointed out to them the unreliability of this 'wisdom', they agreed, but clung tenaciously to their pet beliefs behind my back. Their willingness to agree with me on every point was almost Japanese in its bland and pervasive duplicity.

I had come here hoping to simplify my life, to get down to wood and coal and hammer and brass tacks, as it were, for I have no skill anyway with electronic, electrical, or even mechanical gadgets. These simple, rural folk, on the other hand, had what amounted to an obsession with gadgetry. Once they discovered my electrical drill, for example, I could not get anyone to so much as pronounce 'rawl punch', and in sheer self-defence (or drill-defence) I had to do the hole-drilling myself as they could not be bothered to use different drills for wood, steel or masonry and, contemptuous of such pedantry, happily demolished set after set of bits.

However, my unwarranted pride in my familiarity with such esoteric knowledge, my acquisition of a few letters after my name, and my experience of having knocked about a few countries in the world led me to assume that my rural 'colleagues' would view me with awe, admiration and—I must admit it—gratitude. I pictured myself forever rushing to their aid, smiling benevolently, bottle of iodine in one hand and sack of aspirins in the other. I was also willing, should the occasion arise, to distribute school-books, water purification tablets, sprain balm, mosquito-repellent, condoms. The occasion, alas, never arose, and it took me a couple of blissfully ignorant years to find out that the 'colleagues' did not view me with any sort of feeling at all; and on those rare occasions when I was forced on their view, they saw me as an eccentric but harmless idiot, to be taken advantage of a lot more easily than my neighbours, born and bred to village ways.

All in all, though I did gain clean air, quiet nights, pleasant surroundings, physical fitness, and an extensive though patchy knowledge of fauna and flora I did not achieve a marked degree of success in many of my original objectives in moving here, such as 'improving the lot' of the rural populace and creating in them 'an awareness' of regional, if not national concerns. Though one or two of them did, due to persuasion (it was more like coercion), agree to limit the number of their offspring, none married outside the caste, refrained from taking/giving dowries, or from celebrating weddings/funerals in as sumptuous a manner as they could on money borrowed from me.

Their lives seemed to me to be governed entirely by social or familial pressures and religious observances. Even economic considerations, presumably important in so poor an area took second place to these, for I could never make them see the evil in borrowing money for such extravagances. They would agree that it was foolish to be perpetually in debt for the rigid observance of feasts and fasts but would go right ahead and continue to ask me to lend them money against salaries.

In the end I found myself employing a number of them against my will, so as to pay them salaries which I could cut in order to recover my loans. And naturally, I often found these debtors simply standing around and gazing at the tips of their noses day after day. But I still could not turn them out because they owed me money, which I could not recover unless I paid them salaries which I could cut etc.

In spite of my 'obliging' (read 'gullible') nature, personal loyalty or responsibility played no part in their relationship with me. I found they tended to disappear for days without notice for reasons incomprehensible to me, like attending the naming ceremony of a baby of a cousin-by-marriage-three-times-removed residing in unreachable rural wilderness where even the intrepid state transport made its rattling and mud-or-dust-spattered journey only once a day.

Things, as you have no doubt anticipated, Soon Came To A Pretty Pass. After a couple of years spent in heartbreaking, ceaseless, futile struggle, I was forced to give in on a point of honour. I had to bow to the institution of the mukaddam, an overseer.

Way back when I began my rural venture, and in fact even before that, I had often and loudly denigrated this office. I had said that I would deal directly and openly with all who worked for me without go-betweens. I had claimed that it was people like overseers, those roughneck strongmen and hoodlum middlemen that had sabotaged the economic progress of the subcontinent. I had said I was not going to employ bully-boys to do my dirty work for me in case there was any to be done. My heart was in the right place and my rural employees would recognize that. Sure they recognized it.

And the result of that gleeful recognition was: work never got done, there was a vast number of layabouts on my payroll, and I began to dip dangerously towards red ink.

At last, for the sake of my own economic progress and my tax-accountant's heart, I gave in and decided to employ a man to drive these people who were driving me into the debtors' prison, to do some work; a man, moreover, whose heart they would recognize as not being present in his body. In short, an overseer.

Plainly speaking, an overseer is a bully. You transmit your orders to him (I have never found a female overseer) and he translates them in a forceful manner to your workers. Of course he kisses your ass and kicks the ones of those below him. In the mistaken belief that I possessed a knowledge of economics and sociology superior to my neighbours (all of whom employed one), I had been determined to do without him, thank you. I visualized him wearing knee-boots, wielding a whip and castigated him as an oversure underseer, overrated underdoer, overfed underminer, overpaid underworker...the permutations were endless.

But I was eventually defeated and brought to acknowledge my inability to do without a sort of a filter between me and my workers. However, I was going to stick to my guns about the sort of person I was going to employ. Suspecting some such resolve on my part, friends, neighbours and well-wishers stepped in and firmly found me an overseer who turned out to be, alas, much more firm and much less romantic than myself. Unfortunately he gave no indications of such tendencies in his appearance and I was fooled into giving him the job with a sigh of relief.

He was a youngish, slight, fair man; so fine-featured as to look effeminate. As though to counter such an impression, he had grown a pale and thin moustache which rendered him sufficiently ridiculous to overcome my mistrust. He seemed not capable of wielding any authority, and yet, quite soon a number of tasks which had been dragging got completed within the (admittedly generous) time limits I had set. Urgent projects such as ploughing before rains were started. And most importantly, nose-gazing people disappeared to be replaced by another lot bearing a marked resemblance to the overseer. He told me mildly, upon inquiry, that those people had been taking advantage of my good nature and he could not allow that. He said it so mournfully, he practically brought tears of gratitude to my eyes and it took me quite a while to realize that it was a variation upon the old 'not to bother your pretty head about it all' which, when said by me used to bring tears of rage to my wife's eyes.

It is true that after his advent things went on a lot more efficiently and perhaps more profitably too, but I was strangely unhappy. I had nothing to do but walk around importantly and be 'consulted' about various matters in which I found myself agreeing with whatever plans he had made. I suppose it was polite of him to 'consult' me. And in fact he was a most polite fellow. He always listened with great seriousness to the gibberish I spouted about the Necessity of Doing Away with Superstitions and the Caste System. He never bullied anyone that I could see and he hardly ever raised his voice to any of the workers. I could not guess at the source of his undoubted authority. Certainly it wasn't I, because if I had it to give, then I would have had it to wield.

After some time spent puzzling over this phenomenon, my curiosity got the better of me and I inquired of the neighbour who had recommended this overseer so highly. He laughed and said, 'It's quite simple. Tell me, what's his name?' 'His name? Oh, Thus-and-so,' I replied even more mystified. 'There you have it.' 'What?' 'The source of his authority. That name owns just about everything around here. If you go far back into who actually owns the land you sit on, you will probably find that *he* does, or his father does, or his brothers, uncles, cousins, whoever. It's all a matter of his caste and his family, you know.' Profoundly shocked and saddened, I wondered how I could regain the reins of my own life from the hands of this perfect monster disguised as a pretty little man with a silly little moustache who was, as I had always suspected, the embodiment of all that is nefarious in Modern India.

I soon came to realize that getting rid of him was beyond my capacities. In fact, in an ever-smiling, mild and deferential way, he seemed to relegate me more and more easily to the status of a supernumerary. The 'discussions' of work-to-do every morning became recitals of what he meant to do and the 'reports' of what-had-been-done at the end of the day deteriorated into a ritual leave-taking or admiring-the-sunset. I consoled myself by reading Thomas Mann, Dostoevsky and Dickens. I made trips to the town to see movies. I wrote lengthy letters to faraway friends. I yearned for unexpected visitors and the absent wife and children. I decided to write a novel. I took long walks and collected microliths. I looked back longingly upon the early years when I could not fit all I wanted to do in twenty-four hours and came home every evening from the fields tired, dirty, frustrated, poor and happy. I began to loathe the overseer for making my life full of ease and leisure and free of economic worries and petty setbacks.

He did not really need me except to hand over the payroll bag to him every Saturday when he presented me with the muster book. If I decided to walk through the fields where work was under way, he would hurry over and patiently answer every stupid question with smiling ease. If I didn't like or believe what I was told I had no means of showing my displeasure effectively. I took it out on him by needling him in petty ways. This made me thoroughly ashamed of myself, especially when he quite meekly agreed to change the brand of fertilizer being used in my microscopic kitchen plot and to substitute the lazy woman weeding my futile and risible flower garden. Everyone got on fine without my inexpert forays into matters really agricultural. Even I got on better without them. But success and ease made me furious because I knew it was all wrong; I had simply been manoeuvred into an ideologically false and existentially anomalous position by this smiling doppelgänger.

My researches had shown that he had indeed owned, or part-owned this tract of land and was now sitting pretty because I was paying him to work his own land and supplying him with a labour-force and seed and fertilizer he could not have afforded earlier. He was no worse off than before when he probably got no more than a couple of bags of sorghum out of it after hard toil. He now got the couple of bags of sorghum as well as a salary and a fiat to boss everyone in my name. Yes, I was furious and still I went placidly on my long walks and read my Tolstoy late into the night. My real frustration was, no one could see any reasons for me to be so unhappy. They congratulated me on possessing such a treasure. And I went around fuming and wishing someone would steal this treasure from me because I had not the courage to get rid of him. The soft life

Morgan in Disguise 173

had demoralized me within one year of his arrival as he had known it would.

In a fit of temper I said to the neighbour who had recommended the overseer, 'He is nothing but a highwayman, a robber, a bandit, a pirate!' and the neighbour turned around and glanced at him across the veranda. The pirate was economically and busily directing others to direct water into the proper channels for my newly planted trees, keeping an eye on the correct amount of industry displayed by a couple of ditch-diggers and saying something pleasant to the giggling girls weeding nearby. This picture of exemplary and totally un-pirate-like activities evoked what was almost a giggle from my neighbour too, which he hid in his beer as he chided me with, 'Come on! He is a perfectly nice fellow and quite devoted to you, you know! You are lucky to have him. Admit it now!' But glaring at that offending slender back I declined to admit anything of the sort.

On Sundays everyone took off for the market. I stayed home with my Dickens, and enjoyed being 'Lord of all I surveyed', since, for that one day, 'all' did not hold my overseer. But that Sunday I was not so lucky. Around noon when the frenzy of the bazaar and the heat of the day were at their height; when I expected to be left alone to my one blessed carefree day and one blessed pre-lunch cocktail, I discerned him cycling towards my house. By the time he clambered up the steps he was bright red and running with sweat, and I noticed him tenderly cradling a small tote-bag.

I assumed it to be an offering from the market of vegetable marrows, fresh ears of corn or a watermelon and said 'thank you' a little dryly when he proffered it. But the little bag was light and warm and emitted a sort of a snuffle. Startled, I nearly dropped it and neatly retrieving it he smiled and said, 'It's a puppy. Our bitch has just littered so I thought I'd bring you one—for company.' I was speechless with a mixture of emotions I could not begin to analyze. He widened his grin, put his hand in and brought out a milk-smelling, puppy-smelling, chubby, white mutt with black patches all over it. When he saw that I still didn't say anything, he went on, with a little laugh, 'I thought we'll call him Pirate—on account of the eye-patch you see.' And, staring at the puppy with the eye-patch and the Overseer without, I too, began to laugh at last.

Dmitri in the Afternoon

ULKA thought it a tremendous stroke of good luck that she should have this opportunity to go to Greece with her husband. And that too, in the summer break. But then all her life she had always been astonished by her good luck. Her mother had once said laughingly that she must have accumulated a lot of good karma to be born so lucky. First of all there was her great good luck in being born at all. Her parents had almost given up hope of a child when she was born and so it didn't matter to them that she was not a boy. They were thrilled with her, a bit red and wrinkled and bawling, but a perfect baby nevertheless.

They adored her and spoiled her and granted her every wish. She grew up never knowing the meaning of disappointment, sorrow, anguish or depression. When, after college, she wanted to specialize in some esoteric new science, they didn't say a word. And then she wanted to teach so her father dropped the right word in the right ear and got her a post. Then she 'fell in love' with a man not of their community and they swallowed all their opposition and she was married to him in a swirl of silks, a blaze of jewels, a burst of fireworks, a glut of feasts and a symphony of music just as if they had chosen him themselves. And then came the babies...a girl and *a boy*! Her mother could have sprouted wings and flown for joy.

Those two apples of their grandmother's eye could certainly not be taken to some outlandish country. If Ulka wanted to follow her husband—the son-in-law whom her mother had come to love over the years—she might go, though her mother wasn't too sure about that either. Ulka was dismayed. 'But Mum, Greece! The Isles of Greece and the wine-dark seas and the Parthenon and Corinth and Thebes and Delphi... Just imagine, darling! I could be putting my foot in the exact same spot as...as Pheidippides in Marathon!' Her father smiled, but her mother thought that maybe she had become a bit foreign, just like that quiet husband of hers. Aloud she said, 'You can go if your husband wishes it, but you leave the children with me. They are too young to go junketing about the world; and besides, they've both inherited your delicate stomach.' She had in fact never suffered from a single ailment of the alimentary canal, but her father winked at her and she kept quiet. She was a little apprehensive about what Denzil would say to leaving the children behind, but he only laughed his utterly adorable, one-corner-of-the-mouth laugh and said, 'Well, if the old folk want the children to themselves for a few months, then I can have *you* all to myself for a few months.' And he kissed her in a prolonged and preparatory sort of way.

So here she was, actually in Athens. She could hardly believe that every morning when the smog and pollution were not too thick, she could see the Parthenon glinting in the sun. And the people! Their golden perfection and ready friendliness took her breath away. Every day she quickly rushed through the household chores and made her way to the yacht marina where opulent boats with lyrical names swayed at anchor and the sailors working on them pretended to ogle her. She knew it was all a game, for who would really ogle *her*, a wife these ten years and a mother of two? But she always laughed and waved.

Or she strolled to the harbour to see ferries leave for Lesbos, Rodos, Kriti, Korfu... Then there was the beach, the startlingly purple-blue sea and hot golden sands. Sometimes she just wandered over to the café above the market and sat in the sun feasting her eyes on the descendants, she was sure, of Hercules and Achilles and Ulysses and the glorious Helen.

She had never had any occasion to wonder if she herself were good-looking or not and so could unenviously and wholeheartedly wallow in the pleasure of the sight of these golden lads and lasses. Of course she had been assured many times by her parents and Denzil that she was the most beautiful thing on earth, but she didn't take them seriously. She did think she could not be so bad, because after all so wonderful a man as Denzil loved her; but that too, she supposed, was part of her good luck. After a decade of unmitigated marital bliss she still felt she was very lucky to have him love her. Well, perhaps not as much as she loved him, but a lot nevertheless. And he seemed to love her more since they came to Greece, which was only natural, because here the air was like magic, the sea incredible, the food fit for the gods and the scent of sage and thyme perfumed even smog-choked city streets.

In a sort of a happy fog herself, she walked, or sat in the cafés, or idled by the shops before going home in the late afternoon to begin dinner. She even chopped onions in a mist of love because *he* was going to eat them and then he was going to smile at her across the table his conical, glancing smile and say, swirling the pale golden wine in its cold, misted glass, 'Did I tell you today, sweetheart, I adore you?'

How in hell did I get to be so bloody lucky? she thought that morning, looking at the murky coffee in her cup while she sat at the little sidewalk café before beginning the long ascent home after her morning stroll. She had picked up a lot of speech habits from Denzil such as the occasional swearword and tended to use a few rough and masculine phrases when her parents were not by to keep her to the strictly correct ladylike speech they had drilled into her. She must have smiled at herself remembering her father's frown at such lapses and the woman at the next table must have taken it as a friendly overture, because she smiled too and said, 'Hello!'

Ulka, lost in her own daydream was startled, but also smiled and said, 'Hello,' right back, being in charity with the whole world.

The woman, about her own age and marvellously handsome and glamorous, picked up her cup and, saying, 'May I?' got up and came to Ulka's table.

Before sitting down, she asked, 'That's a wonderful dress you are wearing; what is it called?'

'Sari,' Ulka said, and added, 'do sit.'

The woman smiled, sat down, and said, 'I am Maria Aristides.' Ulka laughed and introduced herself and Maria asked why she had laughed. Still laughing Ulka said, 'You know, I expected all of you to be called Andromache and Clytemnestra and Aphrodite and Athene.' Maria laughed too, and said, 'Well, I expect Christianity changed all that and now we're called Maria and Nicola; Alexandra and Olga. Nothing as dramatic as Andromache, I'm afraid.' They both laughed and exchanged pleasantries about each other's countries and situations and the weather, until Maria happened to glance behind Ulka and broke into a rather mischievous smile of welcome.

Now Ulka looked back too and there was a dark, rather stocky and annoyed-looking man standing behind her. Maria said, 'Hello, love. Ulka, I want you to meet my brother Jack.' Before she could help it, Ulka exclaimed, 'Oh, no!' And both brother and sister were quite taken aback. Realizing her rudeness and laughing a little, she explained, saying, 'How do you do? I am sorry, but I am totally disappointed in your name! You could at least have been Vassili or Constantine or even Alexander; but Jack! I can't allow that.' Jack came up to the table and pulling out a chair, said, 'I've got a lot of those sort of names too, but Maria calls me Jack because she knows it annoys me. How do you do? Are you visiting here?' But then, not waiting for an answer, he turned to his sister and said something quite sharply in Greek. Ulka felt acutely uncomfortable and wished she hadn't given in to her feeling of universal brotherhood when she asked Maria to sit down at her table. Now her morning was likely to be spoilt by a family squabble among strangers. She pushed her own chair back to make an excuse and leave. But Jack turned to her and said with a smile that put an unexpected dimple in his bristly dark cheek, 'I am sorry; I did not mean to be rude to you, but I reminded my sister that she is quite remiss in idling her time away here when she had agreed to meet me in our lawyer's office.' Maria said, 'Now Jack, you know quite well that you made an appointment to meet me *here*. I was a little early and when this exotic and beautiful blossom smiled at me, I couldn't resist her. Can you?'

At once bewildered and pleased at this speech, Ulka blushed and looked down into her empty cup. To her relief, Jack laughed, forgetting his annoyance, and said, 'My dear sister, go on to Costa's office right now and sign those very important papers, otherwise I will be seriously annoyed with you.' Collecting her bag from under her chair, she stood up and smiling again her mischievous smile, said, 'I can see that, Jack. Goodbye, Ulka. Take back happy memories from my country that will make you younger every time you remember them.' Enchanted by this new variation of the plain 'goodbye and have a good time', Ulka also smiled wholeheartedly, forgetting that this was a perfect stranger, and said, 'I most certainly will, especially of friends like you. Thank you, Maria.'

And just as she was preparing to say a similar goodbye to Jack too, he called the waiter and ordered more coffee and asked her a shade abruptly, 'What would you have me called?'

'What?'

'You seemed very disappointed in my name; so what would you have me called, if not Jack?'

'How about Pheidippides?'

Now he laughed in real amusement and said, 'I can see you are a tourist. No one is called anything like that any more. Most of us are Giorgos and Aleko and Niko and Dmitri.'

'Well, I guess, I could settle for Dmitri.'

'Very well then, you may call me Dmitri, because it *is* one of my six names!'

She wondered why she should call him anything at all, when in all probability he would vanish out of her life as soon as she got up and walked away. Sensing her withdrawal, he said, 'Allow me,' and poured some more coffee in her cup. She was looking down at it, wondering again why she lingered on, when she felt his eyes on her and looked up, almost reluctantly, knowing what she would find in them and feeling again an obscure disappointment.

But he was leaning back and regarding her with a frown of clinical interest. He asked, 'Why did you pick on that particular name? Are you a marathoner?'

'Oh, no, not at all.'

'Why, then?'

'It's just something I said to my mother before...' she trailed off, aware of the impossibility of being able to give him an adequate explanation of this comment. But as he merely continued to wait, she completed her sentence and then added that impossible explanation, and before she knew, had both her elbows on the table and had launched into... But he stopped her with, 'Oh, yes, the wine-dark seas, don't tell me.' He said it in his abrupt way which could have been rude except for that hint of a dimple. He continued, seeing her a little daunted, 'Why don't you come with me and I'll show you what the wine-dark seas are all about?'

Again without waiting for an answer, he put a few coins on the table and stood up with his hand extended, expecting her to put her hand in it and go with him. She took a breath to say, 'I'm afraid I don't have the time; I really must be getting home,' but never said anything at all. Just stood up with her hand lightly resting on his palm and began to walk with him in the direction he took.

He did not take her to the wine-dark seas, which in any case were a sort of a murky turquoise this close to the harbour, but into the small lanes and backstreets and beautiful little tucked-away gardens and brick-paved yards and dark bookshops. Ulka could not have found later the lanes they threaded through.

There were lovely little squares looked upon by dumpy, small, round-domed churches; she was surrounded by whitewashed, vine-or-rose covered houses that sported washing on lines and cyclamens and geraniums on windowsills; she felt cobbles under her feet; smelt the cool scent of anise and thyme, sage and rosemary, lilac and lavender; the hot sun turned her head a little and the taste of the cold, tart retsina in a tiny, dark wineshop made her dizzy with delight as the old men crowding the shop full of tapped old barrels grinned at her. She felt her words wrapping themselves around the sour and creamy taste of feta cheese and Kalamata olives and her questions coming out between sips of biting ouzo. Somewhere along the way she heard the wail of bouzoukia and acquired a bunch of rosemary that Dmitri bought for her in the crowded, smelly, raucous market to scent her fingers that entwined with his, every now and then.

His slightly formal, slightly stilted English fell on her ears like, well, like the wail of bouzoukia, and she found herself waiting for the elusive dimple to appear in his cheek because she never quite believed it would.

And then, they found themselves sitting on a bench in the shade of a lime tree. Right in front of them was a bush that looked like a common Indian tree, the *acacia nilotica*, but it was much smaller. It even had the same little, yellow, fluffy, button flowers. When she asked about it, Dmitri said, it was the *acacia farnesiana*. He got up and picked one fluffy, yellow flower off the bush and enclosed it in his cupped hand. He brought the imprisoned flower near her face and said, 'Breathe in now, breathe in its fragrance,' and opened his hand. She closed her eyes and inhaled, was almost stunned by the rich scent that invaded her senses. She felt she might drown and suffocate, unable to breathe in so much perfume. Almost pleading, she opened her eyes and looked at him.

Help me, she pleaded inside herself. Help me, for I do not know where my years have gone; do not know where I have mislaid my adored husband and children and parents and learning and conditioning. I do not know anything except this drowning. Indeed, I do not know anything at all. Help me not to know. Help me, for you are Pheidippides and Achilles and Alexander and even Jack. Certainly you are Dmitri and I do not want to have knowledge of you. So help me not to know you. Help me.

When he held her face in his hands, she felt the flower, crushed against her cheek. She did not move as he kissed her. His kiss was not the prolonged, preparatory sort of a kiss that she knew quite well. It was entire in itself. An entire and complete communication between two human beings, a statement that did not go on anywhere but began and terminated in itself. A total commitment to that moment of himself in her. And then he stood up and said, 'Have you ever been struck by lightning?' and went away.

It was a long time before she stooped and picked up the little crushed flower, and enclosed it in her fist.

That evening Denzil asked, 'And what did you do today, sweetheart?' And she answered, 'Oh, I wandered around the city as usual and had a cup of coffee at a restaurant and a man called Jack showed me a bush of fragrant flowers that I had never seen before.' 'Did he now?' Denzil said, lifting a corner of his mouth, 'And is that why you have got a smile on your face like the tiger of Riga?' And he tilted her head back with one finger under her chin and kissed her in a preparatory sort of way.

Habits

LIFE depends on certain habits. When there is no reason left to do a thing, no sense in doing it or not doing it, and no one is going to gain or lose anything by your doing or not doing it, then only the habit of doing it will see you through. When one day you get up and begin to wonder why you must brush your teeth, even before the question can be fully formed in your mind, you have finished brushing them from force of habit. Because, a brush was thrust in your hands even before you fully opened your eyes. All such habits sustain persons whose whole lifetime is spent in asking dumb and useless questions like 'Must one always carry an umbrella when it rains?', 'Must one sleep when night falls?', 'Must one feel aroused instead of disgusted when one sees one's wife asleep with widespread legs?',

'Must one always love one's children?' and so on. The inevitable downstream speed with which these persons have landed themselves in circumstances which generate such questions usually carries them through it, and before they can ask whether one must die, the habit of living has killed them, once and for all.

By the time I met him, I had already formed the unfortunate habit of loving a dumb rascal, otherwise, I must admit, he was just the kind of person I could easily have fallen in love with. Skinny, long-nose, green-eyes and wild. At this point, there was a violent clash between his habit of making women fall in love with him and my habit of being in love with only one person at a time. We made our life a miserable hell, so much so that the rest of our friends started worrying about us. In the meantime, the dumb rascal that I loved went and secretly got married to another woman. But that is another long story.

Anyway, finally, in a fit of rage, the green-eyed one left me for good. But, of course, by then, I was used to having him chasing me around. So then I brooded and sulked, sent him a couple of stupid letters, didn't allow anyone else to grab the phone for a few days (got blasted by my brothers and sisters for doing that), went wandering all over town in the hope of catching a glimpse of him, and committed other such follies.

But all this happened a long time ago, and, the point is that since then, I am thoroughly alarmed at the prospect of forming a habit. Any habit. I gave up doing things punctually just so as not to fall into that habit. I gave up many people that I liked, because I didn't want to get addicted to them. I married someone I did not particularly care for—a person, moreover, whose job sent him out of town frequently. Even my children I loved only off and on. In short, I became a rather peculiar and unreliable sort of person.

Of course, as a result of such erratic behaviour, I became terribly skinny as well (since I did not want to form the habit of eating a square meal), most of my teeth rotted in my head and sported cavities, people started referring to my husband as 'poor fellow' and my kids as 'poor kids'. No one actually tried to put me in the madhouse, only because, to all appearances, I was well educated and more or less functional. However, that 'poor' husband of mine, who at first was attracted to me because he thought I was 'different', finally got fed up and left me. Then of course, I had to start working to support myself and the 'poor kids'. Since no one besides myself had any fear of habits, but, on the contrary, seemed to rely on them, I had to surrender to the tyranny of several dangerous habits such as going to work at a certain hour, coming home at a given time, taking the kids to school and picking them up on time, and so on.

You must have gathered by now that our real story starts at this point. There are plenty of snares in this world to catch a person so eccentric. And plenty of people to lead them on. In fact, many souls actually believe it to be their sacred duty to 'help'. One such soon came my way. Now this fellow was not like that one—the one with a long nose, green eyes, etc. God knows where that one went. I have never seen him again to this day. (If I do see him at all, I would like to salute him as my guru. You will soon find out why.) So this one said to me one day, 'What time are you usually home?'

About fifteen years had passed since anyone had asked me such a question and gotten a straightforward answer. So at first I did not know what to say. (In fact, since I was so skinny and rotten-toothed, no one ever thought of asking me any questions.) Besides, since I was against forming any habits other than the absolutely essential ones, I never used to stay at home at a certain time anyway. So I said without thinking, 'After six.' This was perhaps not so peculiar an answer because he smiled modestly (he is one of those), and went back to work.

Then, for some days, I avoided staying at home after six. But when I realized that I had formed a habit of going for a walk every day after six, I got alarmed and stayed home, and sure enough, he caught me at home. He said that he was in the neighbourhood to see someone, and had just dropped in to see whether I was home.

(After he had gone, the kids said, 'Mom, this gentleman has been coming by all week.' Right then I should have recognized him as The Enemy.) I smiled showing my rotten teeth, and gave him coffee, and then he settled down to talking. He said that he had a certain doctor and that he went to this doctor for a regular check up every six months. (My God!) He also told me the name of his dentist. He stated sorrowfully that he had noticed how I don't always eat lunch, so he promised to take me for lunch the next day to his usual lunch-room where he had his usual table and waiter. I learned how two years ago someone had dared change his usual coffee mug and substitute another one in its place, and how he had given them hell over it. And of course I learned that he had never been late to work, not even once, in the ten years he had worked at our firm, so that the G.M. had made special mention of him in the last annual report. I said, 'Why, then people must be setting their watches by your comings and goings!' And he said, 'That's exactly what I was going to tell you next!' I kept staring at him wide-eyed, as if he were a rhino in a zoo. Then he left.

While saying goodbye, he said to me, 'See you tomorrow.' At that I was really alarmed. Imagine! I had been trotting off to work all this time every day at the same time! It was terrifying that someone should actually take it for granted that he would see me the next day at work. I stayed home. He showed up after six, saying worriedly, 'I hope you're not sick.' I said, 'Of course not. I just got bored with work so I stayed home.' He said, this time perplexedly, 'How can you do such a thing?' and instead of sitting down, began to wander around the room distractedly.

The kids had just left to go to my sister's for the holidays. The house was a mess. He casually started picking up newspapers and folding them in neat piles. The alarm bells rang again in my mind and I said, 'Let's get out of here, shall we? I'm bored sitting at home all day long.' He agreed to that. When I put on my sandals, he said, 'Why don't you wear that green sari, it looks so nice on you.' (Tactful way of suggesting that I change out of my deplorably shabby and crumpled outfit, one must admit.) Of course I paid no heed. While we were walking along, harmlessly enough I thought, he suddenly let loose a diatribe: 'You just don't take proper care of yourself. It is obvious to me, that you don't seem to have a sense of identity, a sense of pride in yourself. (Dear me!) You have never asked yourself the questions: Who am I? What is my place in this world? What is my function? (Of course I don't ask myself such questions. What a waste of time asking oneself questions to which one hasn't got answers. Why not go to sleep instead?) Think about this: how would the world go on if people started to stay home just because they got bored with work? (Why does the world have to go on? Let it go to hell.) One must discipline oneself so as to be able, in times of stress, to live on the strength of that discipline.' (Why? One mostly manages to live on the strength of the fact that one is born.)

Then suddenly turning towards me, he said, 'I have seen you for the last two years, four months and thirteen days, ever since you started working for us. You don't make friends with anyone, don't mix with anyone, it's just you and your work. You are so good-looking (what!), but you dress so carelessly, so shabbily (that's true enough), I feel so much for you. I have been thinking for days. I have been very upset for the past several days. Finally I made up my mind. I have to talk to you. Don't say anything now. Think. You've formed the habit of living your life in this manner. So you won't be able to change it suddenly. I don't want to hurry you. But you should think about it. I can't bear this uncertainty any longer. Your nature is such that you might even give up this job one day, saying that you got bored with it. And I am so used to seeing you, talking to you, that I won't be able to take it. I am aware of the fact that life has dealt you a terrible blow (my knees were about to buckle at this point thinking of such a blow, before I pulled myself up, asking, what blow?), so someone must look after you and the children. I want to do that. You are so young, so sad, so vulnerable (good grief!)... Think, think about it.' Then he turned, and marching with military precision, disappeared.

I had been staring at him open-mouthed all this while, which means he must have clearly seen all my rotten teeth, chapped lips, dandruffy, dirty and tangled hair, hollow cheeks, bags under eyes, and picked pimples. And yet the poor soul had said all that. I really started to feel sad and vulnerable and young and mistreated by life. I thought, I really must get a haircut. And get that green sari dry-cleaned. Wonder if the old iron is still working? What did he say was the name of his dentist? Maybe I should wear lipstick to work and take it with me to lunch for a touch-up. Better go home and clean up the mess because he is sure to show up tomorrow after six...

There I stopped with a jolt. 'Hail the green-eyed guru!' I said, and sent a telegram to my sister, 'Arriving tomorrow'.

Translated from the Marathi original 'Savay' by Vidyut Aklujkar and the author.

Brand New Pink Nikes

It was a long time since she had bought herself a new swimsuit. She knew the old one had become mouldy, but couldn't summon up enough energy to go shopping for a new one. She might not have bothered until the old one sort of fell apart, but her daughter came over for a holiday and said, 'Come on, Mum, everyone can almost see all the interesting bits!' and so she agreed to buy one. A black one, she thought, and large, so it would cover a lot of ground. Not that she was ashamed of her body. It was a good sort of a body and had stood her in good stead all these years. But she was also a modest person, and though she loved swimming, she was not into showing more of herself than strictly necessary.

Especially not nowadays when a hurried glance at herself in the mirror on her way out had made her exclaim to her husband, 'God, I must lose some weight, I look gross!' He had of course patted her bottom in a familiar way, saying staunchly, 'What rubbish! You look just like you did when I first saw you.' Sadly she had counted off the decades in her mind and given him full marks for goodheartedness but none for honesty. She had also noticed a bit of a—well, face it—sag under her chin which led her, whenever she could remember it, to hold her head a little higher. But generally she was too busy and too full of life to worry about how old she was and how old she was looking and how old she was getting. True, her daughter was just past the quarter century but there were still gallants around who told her they looked like sisters, and wanting to believe it, she did, thinking, I was a girl myself when she was born.

She picked out a large black swimsuit in the department store. Her daughter laughed and said, 'You might think you are about as large as King Kong, but you are only a size twelve after all,' and pulled out one which seemed to her ridiculously small. She went reluctantly into the cubbyhole and stripped. The suit too was reluctant to go onto her sweat-sticky body. She wanted to give up there and then but persisted because she remembered her daughter's laughing face and also the formidable one of the shop-lady who confidently waited for a sale. Cramming herself into the thing, she glanced at the mirror and was dismayed. Granted the light was flat and there was no room to pose advantageously, and the mirror was not used to her reflection (she entertained such whimsical thoughts sometimes when no one was looking), but still...

When had she put on that paunch? And why hadn't her old jeans told her that she had? And what was all that cellulite doing on her thighs? Turning around and craning her neck at an impossible angle, she could see her blue-veined legs and—slack?—behind. She almost burst into tears. Where had all the swimming and jogging and weight-watching gone? Before she could pull the offending garment off her droopy, old, wrinkled, puckered body and hide herself in her baggy jeans again, her daughter said, 'Let me see,' and squeezed in. She gave a delighted hoot, 'Oo, that's great. Très chic, Maman!' In reply, she wiggled embarrassed, staring at the reflected duo. The radiant young beauty next to her, even though she brought a pang of love and pride to her heart because she was her own, could hardly have brought comfort and consolation. Without looking at herself any more, she said, 'All right then, I'll take it if you like it,' and bundled the suit and the girl out and scrambled into the comfortable old clothes that allowed her the illusion of being, if not young, at least not so old. Then she refused to do any more shopping, refused lunch (but felt, what was the point? One skipped lunch could hardly make her svelte!), and kept sneaking glances at herself in shop-windows. Aghast, yet not able to tear her eyes away.

She felt despondent all through the evening, didn't take part in dinnertime banter; an event so unusual as to make her normally non-noticing husband ask, 'Is anything the matter?' And she lay awake a long time after he had fallen asleep and the sounds of distant traffic had stilled.

Of course she knew everyone grew old; just as she knew everyone died. She had seen the slow decline and death of her grandparents, even the not very untimely death of her parents. But then parents, and certainly grandparents were old anyhow, and one was sort of prepared. With a shock she saw herself as an old parent now, and who knew, in a couple of years even a grandparent. Apart from an occasional twinge of fear she had not thought about death. After all, it came and there wasn't much one could do about it. One could not stop one's ongoing life worrying about death. But she had never thought about old age, not in her own context, not in terms of herself becoming old with sagging, wrinkled, puckered flesh, falling teeth, failing eyesight and purse-mouth lips. Death was at least final. But old age seemed to go on and on, getting worse by the minute. Lying here with eyes closed, she was still growing old.

She turned on her side and looked at her husband. In the faint light coming through the curtains, he looked the same as he did on their wedding day. A little grey maybe, a little smelly like a familiar dog, a little snorey...but not really old-looking. Not like her. He had no cellulite on his thighs. No droopy behind and sagging paunch for him. It wasn't fair.

The next morning she pulled on her old shoes, tee-shirt and joggers to go for the usual run, but her heart wasn't in it. When he said, 'You need a new pair of shoes to go with that new swimsuit,' she only replied, 'What's the point?'

That evening they were going out to dinner. Instead of jumping into one of her casually comfortable outfits and slapping on blusher and lipstick anyhow, she spent an hour staring at herself in the mirror, putting on and taking off clothes until he asked, 'What are you doing in there? Come on, we'll be late.'

She emerged carefully made up, and wearing a silk shirt. He said, 'Wow! You look great. Is that a new shirt?'

She did not answer.

He winked at their daughter and said, 'Wonder who she's going to meet at that party.'

The girl, halfway out of the house on the way to another party, laughed and waved, but the mother could not raise a smile. She had a terrible time at the dinner. Everyone seemed so oblivious, so glittering and confident, full of plans, scintillating with witticisms and burbling with laughter that she felt flattened. The wine was like medicine in her mouth and the food like lead. What was she doing among all these zappy, zesty, beautiful young things? Sitting and smiling, dutifully making the right responses like a zombie? Finally she found herself making a sharpish response to Jinder's usual nonsense and regretted it when his round, cheerful face creased in puzzlement. Who can say, she then thought, unbeknownst to me, inside themselves, all my friends and acquaintances could be as desperate; they just manage to put up a better front than I do.

On the way home, she was silent, pretending to doze.

Her husband said, 'That was a nice party, wasn't it? And I could see everyone admired your new image. What's next on the shopping list? A string of pearls?'

Irritated, she again found herself saying sharply, 'Can't I buy a new shirt without being told my image needs renovating? And who cares about the admiration of a bunch of hicks anyhow?'

She regretted this too, when he returned no reply, perhaps hurt. But he ought to be used to her sharp tongue by now, she thought; and then said a little contritely, 'I'm sorry. I've not been feeling up to things.'

After all, it wasn't his fault she was growing old. Wasn't anybody's fault. Or perhaps the earth's fault for turning round and for pulling down her once-enviable bust towards her knees. The only reason it won't reach my knees, she thought bitterly, is because my paunch is in the way!

That night too, it was a long time before she fell asleep. She was surprised at herself. Normally she wasn't given to wondering what she looked like. Brought up by parents who were a bit strict and straight-laced she was always told, 'handsome is as handsome does.' She had believed it, being generally satisfied with what she did. Even as a young woman in her prime she had not been given to vanity. Now she thought, Where was the time? I was too busy doing things, too involved in life and work. Where did all the years go? How did I get here without ever having been there, where everyone was once young and pretty? She did remember a few admirers, a few moonlit nights, a couple of besotted youths that she had laughingly turned down, a few sky-highs that had ended in thumping falls when she realized that the objects of her adoration were unaware of her existence.

But she had forgotten it all, perhaps a bit wryly but certainly without regrets. Mostly she remembered fun, laughter, earnest conversation and being busy-busy-busy. What was I so busy with, she wondered. Like a marathon-runner, she seemed to have decided to complete the course without paying attention to the scenery on the way. And here she was, past the halfway mark, and the only one, it seemed, who had noticed that the landscape had changed. From beautiful to bleak, from stimulating to stark... She dreamt listless dreams that night, fell into a deep doze towards morning and did not get up in time to go jogging and assuaged guilt by saying dully to herself, 'What's the point?'

She was afraid her daughter would insist on taking her swimming in her new suit, but fortunately she had other plans. They arranged to meet in the afternoon at a favourite café and do a bit of window-shopping. She was a little early. Instead of going inside and consuming unwanted cups of coffee while waiting for a girl notorious for being late, she chose to stand under the awning, watching the crowd flow by. Remembering an article on how to make every moment count in your fight with flab, she humorously thought she might usefully employ this time in improving her posture or doing some unobtrusive isometrics to tighten her abdominals. She was feeling a little less despondent, mainly because she had taken care not to glance at herself in the ever-present mirrored windowpanes. And so this thought did not bring this morning's hopeless 'what's the point?' to her mind, but a bit of a smile as she straightened her spine and tucked in her gluteals and thrust out her pelvis in the approved fashion.

Seeing her smile, a man standing nearby, obviously a lost tourist, smiled right back and asked hesitantly, 'Excuse me, ma'am, but do you speak English?' Not having been aware of his presence so near, she was a little startled but replied politely, 'Yes, can I help you?' 'Sure is good to hear the old familiar words!' the stranger, an American wearing a camera and a print shirt said, relieved. She managed to tell him the way to wherever he wanted to go and expected him to thank her and wend his way; instead he asked, 'Could you consider having a cup of coffee with me?' Quite taken aback and not knowing how to snub him politely, especially as she was waiting in front of a café in order to have a cup of coffee, she smiled again and was nudged towards a table. When her daughter arrived fifteen minutes later, she found a large, friendly stranger shaking her mother's hand, preparing to depart and then turning back with a smiling and admiring glance before exiting. She also found her mother laughing, something she had been missing for a day or two. There seemed to be an underlying irony in it, but the laughter was back again, thank heaven.

That night her husband found her surprisingly responsive, and was happy enough to benefit without wondering why. He supposed that these strange swings of mood were normal at her time of life but he was too wise by now to say such things out loud, too well-versed in the tact that makes matrimony work. As she lay awake beside him later, conforming to what seemed to her to be a developing pattern of insomnia, she felt herself begin to shake with a fierce, consuming compassion for him. She had sensed his surprise at her overture and also his suppression of the joking question that must have arisen to his lips. Hearing every quiet, sleeping breath he drew, she thought of how sad his fate was. Poor man, forced to make love after putting out the light, to her dull, loose-skinned, ageing body; happy at the small crumb of her occasional enthusiasm, awakened in her not by himself but by a chance encounter with an admiring stranger. Oh, poor, sweet man; with his endless tact, a kind of an absent-minded gallantry and cheerful familiarity that allowed him to love and cherish her year after year, not minding that she was getting so endlessly old and crumbly.

Perhaps he did mind it? If he did, then he was almost heroic. In an everyday, casual, humdrum, unaware way, but heroic nevertheless. She wished she could express her admiration, pity, sorrow, understanding; all this pure and aching feeling which was perhaps stronger than the love which she had almost come to assume she felt for him. She did remember quite clearly that some time, early on, she had been 'in love' with him, doing the usual 'in love' things like falling on his neck every evening when he came home from work and working herself up into tears at longer separations. But, slowly along the way they had settled down to a peck on the cheek and 'Hi, I'm home, what's for dinner' and 'Did you remember to pack the cold tablets' and 'I'll probably go straight to the office from the airport' and only sometimes, 'Good to hear your voice' and hardly ever, 'Love you,' because, she thought, surely, it was to be assumed at last.

And now, surprised at the terrible strength of this new feeling which was so like love, so like what she had felt when she first held the babies to her breast, she turned into his sleeping shoulder and preventing herself from crying for fear of waking him, fell asleep.

The next morning she did get up in time to go jogging and it didn't at all occur to her to think, 'what's the point,' and they said 'good morning' as usual to other joggers and wondered if the Williamses could be invited with the Joshis for dinner next Saturday and she said, 'It doesn't do to mix Europeans with Indians because then the menu is a problem,' and he said, 'Also because we all tend to lapse too often into Hindi or Marathi and that's not fair. But we do need to call the Williamses before they go on holiday,' and she said, 'Well, whatever you say then, because you are the boss,' and both laughed because it was blatantly untrue and glaringly obvious.

Coming home sweat-drenched, she bent down to untie the shoelaces and said, 'You are right. These bloody shoes have got a case of 'galloping grungs'. Why don't I buy a pair of those brand new Nikes everyone is raving about?'

He said, 'Why not add a pair of pink shorts while you are about it?'

Their daughter, coming out of the bedroom, rubbing sleep out of her eyes heard this and said, 'Hey, I'm taking you swimming today in the new suit; all these pink Nikes and pink shorts we can get tomorrow.'

Picturing her in that outfit everybody started to laugh.

Afterword

THERE is the theory of literature. And then there is the practice of it. These days the autonomy of literary theory often overshadows the intricacies of literary practice, which it is perhaps meant to explicate. The stories in this book almost do not seem to need any theory to vindicate them; they speak for themselves. The normal process is thus reversed. Whereas theories are used to interpret literature, the points of view expressed in these stories may themselves constitute a theory. Gauri Deshpande's life and writings are an extension of each other, a part of an ongoing process; separate the two and you have an incomplete understanding of both. It is in this context that I would briefly like to look at some of the stories, identify the author's recurring concerns, and show, by implication, how they are a throwback to the primal impulses in Gauri.

Take 'The Lackadaisical Sweeper' where Narain does not give a fashionable new name to his wife Seeta after their wedding, but she is in no position to do anything about it. It is reported ironically that by retaining the name Seeta, Narain wants her to emulate a goddess, a mythical-allegorical being devoid of female sexuality and humanness. In truth Narain wants her to be no more then a domestic slave. Seeta has been raised to believe that 'no husband wants a skinny scarecrow for a wife.' But it doesn't occur to her that the reverse could also be considered: how does a wife want her husband to look? Similarly, when it comes to the issue of having children, it is Narain who decides that he doesn't want any for at least three years. Seeta, in whose womb the baby will grow, isn't in the picture at all.

In 'Rose Jam', being a good cook is described as an essential qualification for Indian women. However, the narrator proclaims with relish that neither of her grandmothers was much of a cook, and speaks at some length of their haphazard cooking. In fact Aai, her mother's mother, comes across as an atypical Indian woman; and so does Baya, her father's mother, who regretted never having had a daughter and so adopted many. Pride in the girl-child is a recurring theme in Gauri's writing.

Gender-relations are wittily described in 'A Harmless Girl', in which the narrator who is hyper-silent to the point of absurdity falls in love with the 'noisiest, brashest, heartiest, laughingest man anyone had ever met.' Noise here becomes a metaphor for all forms of male privilege as if to say that this is how the man is in relation to the woman. Yet there is an ironic twist at the end when the narrator gets pregnant and noisy (powerful?) and a noisy female child is born to her. Though Gauri spares no opportunity to celebrate the birth of the girl-child, it is used here to underline the fact that no one is 'born' a man or a woman: gender and its burdens are acquired as society thrusts us into one or the other role.

Although 'Hello, Stranger!' isn't directly concerned with gender-relations, it has much to say on the subject. The delivery room is called a 'female preserve' and the story asserts that in certain 'preserves' such as child-bearing and labour (and even child-rearing?), the woman is supremely powerful while the man is a helpless onlooker. The man, waiting for the birth of his first child, thinks, 'On the whole, ...daughters demanded less from their parents'— advocacy of the girl-child again. This is also a story that deals with another major concern of Gauri's : a person's (especially a man's) relations with his 'mother' country, a theme recurring in 'Map' and 'The Debt'. One could call it an extension of the 'gender-relations' theme.

The narrator's identification with bit-players in 'Whatever Happened to...' is worth considering. She is fascinated by 'peripheral vision', in the context of bit roles in movies; bit-players are invariably peripheral to the main feature. The relationship between men and women in real life is like that between heroes and extras in reel life. However, as in the case of 'A Harmless Girl', there is a sort of an ironic reversal in this story as well. Gauri takes care to give such twists to her stories in order not to make them propaganda and she does this by a clever manipulation of language and point of view. A concern that has been peripheral in many stories surfaces as a major one here: women's low self-esteem. Lurking in the margins of many stories, this is suggested as one reason for women's marginalisation, for the retreat of even successful, strong women into self-deprecation vis-à-vis any man.

In 'Morgan in Disguise', the narrator refers to the overseer as an 'institution', and thereby brings out his patriarchal nature. Interestingly, the overseer isn't given a name. Nor do we know the narrator's name in this story. Gauri rarely names her male characters; perhaps this is a device by which she intends to allegorize. Even when the subject of the overseer's surname comes up (a surname because of which, the narrator discovers to his horror, the workers listen to the overseer), it is simply spoken of as 'Thus-and-So'. The narrator himself is apparently a naive, urbanised person who finds his illusions peeled away one by one as he contiues to live in his rural fastness. Even his newly learnt lesson about the overseer has to be relearnt, because he isn't 'Morgan in Disguise', but just another human being, a mixture of good and evil. This highlights yet another of her main concerns: a dialogue between illusion and reality.

'Map' is a fine story in which cartography is used as a metaphor for the male gaze; the woman in the story at first gives in to and then subverts the process. As the story nears its conclusion, the narrator becomes increasingly assertive and aggressive. One of the inferences here is that gender rights are neutralised by the sexual dependence of woman on man. One school of feminism therefore has it that only lesbian-feminists can be true feminists. Barbara Ryan speaks of the 'political lesbian' as an ideological category distinct from those women whose natural preference is for people of their own sex. While the narrator doesn't quite come to these conclusions, she does realize that the dependence must end, even if it means replacing the much more flattering man's map of her body with a more honest one drawn by herself. The metaphor in 'Map' becomes all the more interesting when one realizes that the 'narrator woman' is India and the cartographer the imperial power. The epigraph to the story gives us a clue: as we saw earlier, gender-relations on a wider scale.

'Hookworm, Lamprey, Tick, Fluke and Flea' is again what one might call a 'disguised' story. 'Disguised', because under its ironical surface is the 'real' theme: the symbiotic relationship between a parasite and its host. Gauri suggests that women are willing hosts—society has dinned it into their heads that they must sacrifice themselves. As they fall prey to this endless giving, they wake up one day in the middle of their lives to realize that not only have they been sucked dry, but that they have no other option: they can only play host to a variety of parasites.

Having analyzed some of these well-writtten, well-stuctured stories, I would like to say that there is perhaps one drawback in a number of them. In a *Paris Review* interivew, Toni Morrison makes an oft-forgotten distinction between a book and a tract. She says, 'A tract is: 'this is what I believe.' And a book is: 'this may be what I believe, but suppose I am wrong...what could it be?' Or 'I don't know what it is, but I am interested in finding out what it might mean to me, as well as to other people!'

Somehow this sense of uncertainty is lacking in some of Gauri's stories. They are gynocentric; her narrators seem too cocksure of their opinions. (Though as we have seen, she often moves away from stereotypes in the ending of the stories, bringing in an element of surprise and unpredictability.) However, this is an entirely subjective perception, open to debate.

Leaving this flaw aside, there is no doubt that this collection of Gauri Deshpande's short stories in English (she is already an established writer in Marathi) is a significant artistic statement of feminism. No other Indian woman novelist or short story writer in English has so strongly and consistently expressed her anger at the power politics that exist in gender-relations, although Shashi Deshpande's *That Long Silence* and Shanta Gokhale's *Rita Welinkar* may be cited as important examples in that direction, and Suniti Namjoshi's writings display related concerns. While Indian writing in English has several women writers to boast of, not many of them have shown a sustained interest in women's issues; not even the famous quartet, Anita Desai, Kamala Markandaya, Ruth Jhabvala and Nayantara Sahgal, though Desai's earlier work is sometimes 'women oriented'. Gauri Deshpande's is a new, crusading voice that is bound to give an impetus to Indian literature in English.

R. Raj Rao

Other Manas Titles

BHASKARA PATTELAR AND OTHER STORIES

Paul Zacharia

Translated from Malayalam

Paul Zacharia is one of Kerala's best known and admired short story writers. His stories move through a wide range of moods and themes from the gently mocking and teasingly funny to the reflective and even violent. This is the first time a selection of his stories has been translated from Malayalam into English. The title story *Bhaskara Pattelar and My Life* has been made into a film *Vidheyan* by Adoor Gopalakrishnan.

Pages: 246 *Price: Rs. 95.00*

FINAL SOLUTIONS AND OTHER PLAYS

Mahesh Dattani

Mahesh Dattani is one of India's leading playwrights who writes in English. This is the first time a collection of his plays has been published and it includes four of his outstanding works: *Where There's a Will*, *Dance Like a Man*, *Bravely Fought the Queen* and *Final Solutions*.

Dattani's plays are not only clever and witty but wonderfully warm and humane as well. Constantly open to experiment, the plays vary from pure comedy to serious psychological explorations. From the energetic communal clash in *Final Solutions* to the satirical netherworldly manipulations in *Where There's a Will*; from the poetic palimpsest of *Dance Like a Man* to the sophisticated viciousness of *Bravely Fought the Queen*, the plays are a rainbow of motives, emotions and situational undercurrents.

Pages: 404 *Price: Rs. 175.00*

INSPECTOR MATADEEN ON THE MOON

Selected Satires by Harishankar Parsai

Translated from the Hindi by C M Naim

Harishankar Parsai was the doyen of Hindi satirists. For forty years, through essays, stories, novellas and newspaper columns — all running to several thousand pages — he boldly exposed and denounced all that is corrupt and venomous in the Indian body politic, even suffering physical assault in that cause. His sharp pen relentlessly targeted the heartlessness of our caste-ridden society, the vagaries of bureaucracy, the baseness of our politicians, and all the vulgarities and little cruelties that go unnoticed in our daily lives. By turns gently critical, mordantly humorous and downright funny, Parsai's writing is a telling comment on the condition of man. This is the first collection in English of some of his numerous stories.

Pages: 198   *Price : Rs.95.00*

NEERMAI

Na Muthuswamy

Translated from the Tamil by Lakshmi Holmström

Na Muthuswamy, founder member and resident play-wright of the theatre group, 'Koothu-p-pattarai', began his literary career as a highly original and poetic short story writer. Nine of the stories presented here are from those that he wrote during the 1960s and 70s. These unforgettable and beautifully crafted stories recreate in fine detail the richness of life in the village of Punjai, seen from the perspective of modern urban life and its alienating pressures. 'Battlefield', the last and most recent story in this collection, draws on Muthuswamy's folk-theatre experience, and an extraordinary renewal and transformation of this tradition.

Pages : 192 *Price : Rs.95.00*

VAMSHAVRIKSHA

S.L. Bhyrappa

*Translated from Kannada by
the author and Sushuma Chandrasekhar*

Spanning three generations and varied nuances of thought and feeling, *Vamshavriksha* portrays the moral dilemmas that erupt in a small tradition-bound town in Karnataka when long established social patterns are questioned in the name of individual fulfillment. At the vortex of this upheaval is Katyayani who transgresses the taboos against widow remarriage, jeopardising her relationship with her son and linking together the destiny of two emotionally scarred families that are striving to preserve their integrity and their lineage. *Vamshavriksha* is a sensitive exploration of love and loss, of tragedy and triumph, interwoven with spiritual, historical and cultural insights. The film version of this much acclaimed novel won the prestigious Swarna Kamal award.

Pages : 261   *Price : Rs.150*

THE WALLED CITY
Esther David

Vibrant with the sights, sounds and shifting moods of Ahmedabad, the walled city of the title, Esther David's perceptive debut novel traces the rigidly circumscribed lives of three generations of women in an extended Jewish family in the city.

The novel unravels the narrator's struggle to reconcile her Jewishness with the exuberance of the alien ethos in which she grows up and to which she is drawn. While she agonises over life, love and God, rebelling, submitting, groping to find her identity and make sense of her relationships, the rhythm of the city slides into discord as tensions smoulder and old values crumble.

Rich in observation and insight, and written in a highly individualistic style, *The Walled City* is a haunting study of the powerful forces that both unite and divide generations and communities.

Pages : 204   *Price : Rs. 135.00*

A PURPLE SEA

Short Stories by Ambai

Translated from the Tamil by Lakshmi Holmström

The seventeen stories collected here represent the work of the innovative Tamil writer Ambai. Over the past twenty years Ambai has broken new ground, both in terms of fictional forms and the courageousness of her subjects. She has been constantly open to experiment: her stories vary from gem-like prose poems to fantasy and surrealism and to realistic psychological explorations. Well-known translator and editor, Lakshmi Holmström, captures the essence of Ambai's writing for the non-Tamil reader.

Pages : 254   *Price : Rs. 135.00*

For further information about **Manas** books
write to :

EastWest Books (Madras) Pvt Ltd

62-A, Ormes Road, Kilpauk
Chennai - 600 010.